A MAN OF REMARKABLE RESTRAINT

A MAN OF REMARKABLE RESTRAINT

JOHN BRENEMAN

Encircle Publications
Farmington, Maine, U.S.A.

Editor: Michael Piekny
Cover design: Christopher Wait
Cover images © Getty Images

Published by:

Encircle Publications
PO Box 187
Farmington, ME 04938

Visit: http://encirclepub.com
info@encirclepub.com

To Ernest S. Breneman
(1929–2005)
My father

Chapter 1

A light breeze whispered through the trees as Charles walked to the water's edge. His morning stroll to the river was a rare source of relative calm in a troubled consciousness. Since childhood, he'd shared headspace with a volatile alter ego born of a self-preservation instinct sparked by his intense anger-management needs. But in this moment the song of a couple chattering sparrows felt soothing as he inhaled the fresh salt air at a quarter to six in the morning. His timing was good today.

"Ohhhhhhhhhhhhhmmm!"

The drone of the tanker ship's horn was music to his mind's ear—part of a nautical symphony he imagined each time the Memorial Bridge lifted its center span to let a boat the size of two city blocks float into, or in this case, out of town. The bridge offered a clanging of bells (to signal the lifting or lowering of the toll gate arm that halted vehicle traffic on both sides) followed by a siren that reminded him of old gangster movies or a UFO alert. Seagulls scavenging for crabs and discarded scraps from nearby cafés added a screechy chorus. But the heart of his river song was the center span itself. The action of the massive counterweights that raised the bridge's midsection produced an aching, groaning effect that reminded him of whale sounds.

Charles wished he could record these sounds and weave them together into an instrumental jazz composition. He had zero idea about how to edit sound, let alone how to make music from the ideas and imagery that ricocheted around his brain. But his daily walks to and from this spot felt like an involuntary ebb and flow, drawn by the tides to calm his inner noise.

Standing amid the metal benches and tables on the small dock that served as a riverfront pocket park, he walked across the wooden planks and placed both hands on the round black railing, then took a deep breath and gazed down into the water. This was his oasis from the madness, but he also understood that such moments of reverie were a mirage. He clenched his eyes shut and tightened his grip on the railing—then pushed himself back into motion and began walking up the hill toward the center of town.

Portsmouth, his home for the past twenty-something years, gave him a sense of place; and his work as a writer for the local paper gave him a sense of worth. He could see the steeple of the North Church looming above the rooftops of the predominantly brick cityscape. Glancing back at the battleship-gray structure that spanned the Piscataqua River linking New Hampshire to Maine, he flashed back to the story he'd written at the bridge's grand reopening several years ago. The city's beloved former mayor cut the ribbon—just as she had in 1923, at age 5, when the original was unveiled, named in memory of the New Hampshire sailors and soldiers who had given their lives in World War I.

Life. Death. On his good days, Charles thought of himself as part inconsequential speck in the universe, part universal consciousness—existing by happenstance, for now, in a 400-year-old tourist magnet by the sea. His pace quickened as he realized it was almost time to head to the newsroom. Normal people sipped coffee at curbside tables as he walked toward the post office. His jaw clenched when he spotted a little plastic bag of dog shit someone had left by the sidewalk, about 20 paces from a trash can next to the row of mailboxes. He yanked open the door at the blocky, brick federal building that housed the post office and held it for a man wearing a tie who was exiting. But the guy blew right by him as if he did not exist.

"Have a nice day." Charles had mastered the art of emitting those simple words, without betraying the slightest hint of the biting cynicism that echoed through his head or the rage that so often swelled within him whenever people acted like... people. It was almost as if the polite four-word phrase could be pulled, whenever needed, from an unwritten playbook of techniques for channeling the anger within—a mantra of verbal self-discipline crafted to conform to social norms whether uttered in a monotone or with barely veiled contempt.

Etiquette for Borderline Sociopaths, Violence Suppression

Tip No. 7: When angry, to avoid grabbing some jerk by the collar and slamming his face into the nearest car windshield or some other equally self-destructive form of violence, fix one's facial features in a firm yet human-like grimace and repeat after me: "Have. A. Nice. Day." For maximum efficiency, do not add any of your favorite derogatory salutations, including but not limited to: bitch, numbnuts or dipshit; nimrod, fuckwad or dickhead. (For additional terms NOT to use, please refer to Appendix C.)

"I said, 'Have a nice day.'" This time louder, but still without an overt sign of the dark voice shouting at him to clench his fist and swing it. "Yeah whatever, buddy."

The sharp-dressed asshole on the cellphone had brushed past him, eager to hop into his asshole car so he could go cut off a bunch of people in traffic on the way to his asshole job, oblivious to the fact that it would have been nice if he had just nodded, or lifted his chin three-quarters of an inch and made eye contact, to acknowledge the gentleman who had just held the door for him at the post office. Charles' internal voice took charge.

"Sir, it would behoove you to get your affairs in order. Because if I ever see you again, I'm going to pistol whip you with that phone, then jam it into your windpipe, most likely via an emergency tracheotomy performed with a rusty Swiss Army knife."

Yes, politeness was truly dead, having succumbed—some say back in the '70s—to societal trends that tended toward self-obsession. Too bad, because Charles believed basic civility was one of the few things standing between mankind and its, his, innate savagery. But it seemed the threads that held together the fabric of community were irreparably frayed, and this pissed him off. He checked his P.O. box, shredded his daily junk mail with extra enthusiasm, then walked to his car for the short drive to work.

Chapter 2

"On the bright side, there is a severance package."

"Whaaa… Did you say 'severance package'? Because I thought I just heard you say 'severance package.' The way I've always understood it, severance packages are for people who don't have jobs anymore. And I'm pretty sure that when I walked into the newsroom and over to my desk fifteen minutes ago that I had a goddamn job."

His fever rising, Charles felt his body shrinking—as if his unexpected "downsizing" had crossed over into the realm of the physical instead of the metaphorical. Was this really happening?

"Jesus, Katharine. After all we've been through—elections, fires, murders. I mean, our reporting helped the cops lock up the goddamn Oyster Shooter. And this is how it all ends? With 'Can I speak to you in my office' and 'On the bright side, there's a severance package'?"

Charles had devoted himself to The Beacon for two-plus decades, bought a home, set down roots in a routine that reined in his most self-destructive impulses. And now not only was the rug being yanked out from under him, he felt like he was being rolled up in the remnants and thumped with a baseball bat. He thought of the expression: Don't burn your bridges. But his mind was already unmoored and bobbing against the current. Why were his hands suddenly gripping a plunger connected by a wire to a large pile of dynamite—the kind you see in those Road Runner cartoons? Why was he wearing that weird smile as he pressed the handle down into the body of the device? Why wasn't anything happening as the plunger hit the… tick-tick… *BA-BOOM!*

The newsroom, the hallway and half the building exploded—engulfed in a thundering tsunami of searing, rolling, rumbling flames. Smoke alarms wailed. And the presses… stopped. His now-former boss—the woman who had just flipped his world upside-down—was covered in soot, cartoonish wisps of smoke rising from her head and arms as her computer melted into a Dali-esque blob. His eyes stinging, his throat thick and dry, Charles lifted his hand in front of his face and waved away some of the acrid fog. Then, finally, he spoke. "Damn, Katharine," he said, still seething from the impact of having his career ripped away. "You… probably had no choice."

Outside, first responders were surely racing toward a thick technicolor mushroom cloud on the horizon tinged with cyan, magenta, yellow and black from the big barrels of ink down in the press room. Charles just shook his head and looked down. Sure, he felt relieved that his Looney Tunes fantasy was of the Wile E. Coyote variety and not something more hysterically berserk and sinister.

"Good-bye, Katharine," he said as he trudged toward the lobby and out of this place forever. "Charles wait," she called after him. "Charles!"

He felt dozens of eyes on him as he walked out the door. Mitch, the sportswriter who'd once gotten him an interview with Pedro Martinez. Grace, the graphic designer who had let him down easy after he took seven months to work up the courage to ask her out to see "Citizen Kane" at The Music Hall. Allen, the columnist and former editor who'd hired him even though he was so nervous that he knocked over a coffee on the man's desk during the interview. They all watched him, waiting for a chance to offer their condolences and give him a grim pep talk, if only he would look up. But Charles was already gone. He hadn't been the first to get laid off in the ongoing newspaper industry bloodletting, and he wouldn't be the last. When the sunlight smacked his face, he blew out a gut-full of stale air and autopiloted over to his car.

He turned the key and gripped the steering wheel— hands locked at 10 and 2—so hard that his knuckles begin to hurt. Good pain. Then he crept slowly out of the parking lot, focusing on applying isometric tension to his right foot to resist the urge to flatten the accelerator, and pointed his 14-year-old Honda Civic toward home. But when his car came to a stop, he realized he was downtown instead.

Charles had never been a big drinker, but he also had never been booted from his job. In the movies, he figured, the guy usually heads directly to the bar to "drown his sorrows," maybe bend the ear of some sympathetic, world-weary barkeep. The carved wooden sign jutting out over the sidewalk above his head said Mugsy's.

"Mmmm, booze," he thought to himself as he turned toward the door, recalling some lines he'd written for one of his Sunday humor columns: "A new report in the prestigious Imaginary Journal of Medicine reveals that alcohol has been proven highly effective in combating the pain and discomfort often associated with sobriety. Researchers at the University of Maine—Mattawamkeag have found that—in a world gone haywire—moderate to heavy consumption of alcohol provides fast, temporary relief from the ever-present fear of Nazis, dystopian government meltdowns and Lyme disease. Despite its therapeutic efficacy, alcohol consumed for medicinal or recreational purposes may produce a range of side effects including: slurred speech, moronic behavior, loss of driver's license, heightened risk of shouting at the television, delusions of sexiness, general obnoxiousness, nausea and post-traumatic hangover syndrome."

"Gimme a double." His order was met with a hard stare from the bartender. Then an annoyed squint and a shrug. *Um, you're in a real bar, not a movie bar,* Charles told himself. *You can't just say, gimme a double.*

"Bulleit bourbon, straight up. Please." The barkeep obliged, slapping down a coaster and sliding him several fingers of fine brown firewater. Charles nodded and lifted the glass to his nostrils. He breathed in and let the strong fumes tickle his frontal lobe. What the fog just happened!

He figured he was still in shock—both from his actual downsizing and the explosive frenzy of mental images it had triggered. But really, what can somebody say in that situation? Or do? Flip over some tables and cabinets? That's bush league. Punch a wall? Punch a person? C'mon. Envision a frighteningly realistic theatrical conflagration in which every last trace of the former workplace is erased and the bearer of bad news is singed to a cartoonish crisp? OK, getting warmer.

Charles believed gut reactions were best kept close to the gut—permitted to play out in the mind's eye, but rarely shared. A good editor knows how to edit that shit, he thought. Any clown can get laid off and tell his boss to "take this job and shove it." But it takes a true professional to bring to bear the poise and artistry necessary to compose and deliver a more masterful retort, to wit:

Hmm. Downsized, you say? Well, since you have stripped me of my sole, tenuous lifeline to the world at large, I must insist that you ram my former job well up into your tailpipe, through your intestinal tract and stomach cavity, then on up into your esophagus, where it will cut off your ability to breathe, leaving you gagging and flailing for assistance before you topple face down onto the floor, whereupon I will mourn the sad fact that your otherwise comical demise will preclude me from imploring you to kiss my unemployed sphincter.

Charles gazed into his glass, trying to catch a reflection in the amber-colored potion. Head down, he flashed through 14 or 15 thoughts in what seemed like two seconds: What now? I'm getting old. Newspapers are dying. I'm dying. No I'm not. Downsize this. Fire up. Write a book. Fix your resume. Collect unemployment. Lose some weight. Channel the hate. Become a hermit. Shut up. Get a grip.

When he looked up, a guy down at the other end of the bar was staring at him.

OK, still staring. Definitely not very polite, but Charles got the impression this fellow was not the type to be concerned about making other people uncomfortable. This was a job for his inner tough guy. *Hey, pal!* he barked to himself. *You got a problem?*

Charles stared back at the other man—nervous about how long he could hang on without blinking, flinching or crumbling under the pressure of this unwanted showdown with the menacing stranger. Various verbal constructions and visual scenarios rumbled through his mind. As usual, he was in a mood, so he channeled his most confrontational alter ego.

Look friend, where I come from it's rude to stare a man down unless you mean business. So if you don't want me to grab one of these barstools and smash your ugly, pockmarked skull to smithereens... No, wait. Who says "smithereens," idiot? It's not realistic. Blink. Blink-blink. Crap. Now the guy was grinning.

"Hey buddy, what's your poison?" he asked. Before Charles could speak, the guy turned away to catch the bartender's eye. He raised two fingers, tapped his chest and then pointed at Charles' empty glass and his own.

Chapter 3

"How'd you get that one?"

Charles was pointing at the gnarly scar bisecting his new friend's left bicep. "If I told you, I'd have to fucking light you up with my AK and then napalm your ass, Charlie." His laugh boomed like thunder—furious yet frighteningly joyous. "Seriously, it's kinda personal. I'd like to say I got it in a hand-to-hand machete fight with six or seven Viet Cong. But that would be bullshit. And I don't wanna bullshit you, Charlie."

Charles had always hated being called Charlie. But this was different. When this guy said it, it felt cool—like he was being welcomed into the inner circle of the most fascinating character he'd ever met. The man seemed spring-loaded to blurt out absolutely anything. And his tattoos were amazing. On his left arm, just above the secret scar, was one that must have originally said "Question Authority." But the word "Question" was faded, maybe lasered, barely legible—long since replaced with the word "Fuck." Charles theorized that the ink traced an evolution from idealistic

Haight-Ashbury hippie to embittered Vietnam survivor.

Stan seemed belligerent, pissed off—probably haunted by some shit that went down in Khe Sanh or Tam Quan, Hamburger Hill or the Mekong Delta—but also eerily at peace with his own personal hell.

"Whenever the cops ask me for some identification, I just show 'em this."

He pointed to his right bicep. His given name was printed in modest-sized, maybe Franklin Gothic type. But his nickname burst forth, carving a wide arc in thick capital letters, with a drop shadow that gave it a three-dimensional feel. Emblazoned against what looked like a wall of flames were the words Stanley "Apocalypse" Nowell.

Below that was a pretend bullet wound leaking a trail of red ink, a long-haired dude who looked like a cross between Jim Morrison and Jesus, and a grinning reaper—one hand gripping his scythe, the other on the throttle of a Harley.

"This one here," he said, jerking his head toward a calligraphy marking on his left shoulder, "is Vietnamese for 'pussy lover.'" He slammed down his glass, smacked Charles on the back and yelled, "More firewater for me and my friend!" The bartender did not hesitate. "Badass," Charles thought to himself, as he nodded and reached for his glass.

When they finally staggered outside 90 minutes later, the biker threw his arm around the out-of-work newsman and sent him sprawling into a black BMW parked at the curb. The car's alarm went haywire and, as Charles gathered himself, two young men dashed out of an Irish pub to check on the commotion.

"Hey, what the fuck, asshole. That's my car," said the larger of the two.

"Apologies, son. It was an accident," said Stan. "We don't want any trouble."

Joe Linebacker charged right up into his face. "Damn right, you don't. Motherfu…"

Stan's eyes flashed hot and he gave a slight hop as he dropped the taller man with a vicious headbutt. "That's it. Go to sleep, little baby." He looked at the other man, who spread his open hands wide as he took a step backward. "Accidents happen," said Stan.

Stunned, but pulsing with adrenaline from Stan's two-second street fight, Charles glanced down at the lug still slumped by the curb then back at the second guy, thinking, *You want some too, you slack-jawed piece of shit?*

"OK, Charlie. I gotta split. You should too. See you 'round town, amigo."

What? As a deeply introverted, self-styled recluse, Charles had very few friendships, yet a friendship with Stan seemed like one worth having. "Hey, when can we…?" But it was too late, Stan was already gone.

Chapter 4

Charles awoke with what New England drinkers call a "wicked hangover." *Glurtch*. Great way to start Day One of your new, downsized life, he thought. Now that he'd been out of work for 20+ hours, he thought he'd better start scouring the help-wanted ads. His mortgage wasn't going to pay itself. But that could wait a day or two. Worst case, he could look for a housemate to share his two-story, three-bedroom colonial just off Pleasant Street. He snagged it long before the local housing prices went haywire, and loved being able to walk to Market Square and down to the river.

After dry-swallowing two ibuprofen, he dumped some cold water into his $9.88 Walmart coffee cooker, scooped some brown grounds into the filter and flipped the switch. He looked down and smiled. "Good morning, little buddy. You ready for breakfast?"

"Meow."

Every morning, Charles thanked the almost certainly non-existent man or woman in the sky for Elmer, his trusty twelve-year-old side-cat. Ever since the sunny April afternoon he brought the eight-week-old kitten home from the SPCA shelter, feeding the little guy was one of the few activities that made Charles feel like he was contributing anything of value to this ridiculous, ignorant and largely hateful planet.

He opened the cupboard and grabbed a Friskies Savory Shreds entrée from the wide, tall wall of cat food cans that dwarfed his own meager pantry selection—one can each of generic carrots, sauerkraut and 50-cent French cut green beans. Charles felt duty-bound to keep an Armageddon-level supply of pet food in stock because this cat was a stickler for his shreds—would not abide by chunks, and don't even think about serving him that pasty pâté-looking crap. "How about some Turkey & Giblets in Gravy this morning?"

"Meow."

"Meow, you say? I'll take that as an enthusiastic 'Yes please!'"

Using the tarnished silver baby spoon his mother had used to choo-choo train him his Gerber's as a pre-psychotic infant, Charles scooped a dollop of shreds into the blue bowl on the floor and imitated the saliva-inflected inhaling sound the cat emitted as he went to town on his grub.

He cracked open a can of tuna for himself, dropped a pinch in the cat's bowl, and began assembling a sandwich while reflecting on one of his favorite topics, the special joy of an unconditional bond between two beings—one a foot tall, 3 feet when "standing," and weighing in at approximately 10 pounds, 9 ounces; the other 6 feet and one half-inch tall and tipping the scales at maybe 18 times that. Along with offering his daily reassurance that Elmer was indeed his "best friend in the whole wide world," Charles liked to regale his young charge with stories about his infancy.

Elmer had once been skittish and timid in the presence of the foul-mouthed behemoth who raised him. But Charles was proud that he had dedicated himself to nurturing not only the adorable kitten, but also their relationship, determined to forge the most meaningful possible connection with his companion. At the risk of sounding immodest, Charles was obliged to acknowledge that he was—not for the broader feline community, but at least in the case of Elmer—a "cat whisperer." Though he thought the term vaguely pretentious, a bit too precious, he was proud of the work and care he had devoted to cultivating a mutually fulfilling fellowship.

For instance, he had always approached Elmer on the cat's terms—never leveraging his superior size or the advantage of opposable thumbs to impose his affection or will on the smaller party. Knowing that Elmer would quite naturally be wary in the constant presence of a beast nearly 20 times his size, Charles had made it a practice to periodically lie flat on his back on the floor and place the cat on all fours atop his chest, conveying the message to Elmer that he, too, could take a turn as the alpha.

His whisperer self-mediations had occasionally drifted

into contemplation about what other types of whisperers might exist in the human-animal kingdom. So he kept a running list:

- Rattlesnake whisperer
- Snapping turtle whisperer
- Great white shark whisperer
- Komodo dragon whisperer
- Electric eel whisperer
- Portuguese man o' war whisperer
- Red-bellied woodpecker whisperer
- Mud dauber wasp whisperer
- Three-toed sloth whisperer
- Sperm whale whisperer
- Cockroach whisperer
- Porcupine whisperer
- Tasmanian devil whisperer

In exchange for conscientiously carrying out certain responsibilities—chiefly his sanitary duties—Charles trusted Elmer never to abuse the privilege of being granted unlimited 24/7 access to his "crunchies." But, oh, how that cat loved his daily "shreds," delivered into his bowl each morning via his tiny silver feeding spoon. Per their ritual, as Charles would reach into the refrigerator to pull out the can, or crack a fresh one from the cupboard, he would emit a single "meow," to which Elmer would reciprocate in kind.

What then to make of the baby voice? Charles suspected that if Elmer harbored one complaint about their conversational habits, it might be his tendency to talk to him, not quite in a baby voice, but in the tone and inflection of someone who is speaking to a small child. Charles thought of it simply as another way of conveying affection. Oh well, the "little man" of the house seemed unfazed by his cohabitant's peculiarities, though he was known to snap from a lazy nap and bolt for safety when that giant asshole launched into one of his god-awful human thunderstorms.

After he huffed down his grub, Elmer sauntered to the back door, stretched out his front paws, elevated his ass and shiatsu'd the rug with his claws. After breakfast he'd often start acting agitated, pretending his master was chasing him—meaning he wanted to play.

"Little guy never gets to go outside. Here, you want some fresh air?" Charles opened the inside door so the cat could look out the screen door. His multicolored eleven-pound mutt stood tall as he reached his front paws up to peek out the door. "It's a jungle out there, little champ. What do you see?" Trying to imagine himself in a cat's world while stroking Elmer behind the ears, Charles let his eyes follow a butterfly, then a pigeon, then... the phone rang.

"Hello?"

"Good morning, sir. I'm calling with a very special offer for first-time subscribers to the *Portsmouth Beacon* newspaper. For the low introductory price of just..." Charles smashed the hard plastic receiver of the land line he meant to get rid of six months ago down onto a pile of bills on his kitchen counter, then initiated the three-count/

inner dialogue process he sometimes used to allow his rage to diffuse before speaking.

One. *"Are you fucking kidding me!?"* he did not yell out loud.

Two. *"News flash! The owners of that abominable rag put a knife in my back yesterday, so I'd rather soak the Sunday edition in gasoline and torch the place than purchase a subscription!"* he almost said.

Three. OK, breathe. "Really, that's a very interesting coincidence because I just got laid off after spending nearly half my life working at that fine publication," he told the caller. "So, thank you, but I'm afraid I'm going to have to pass on your subscription offer." Elmer was up in the loft now, peering down through the slats in the railing. "It's alright, little pal," Charles told him. "Nothing to worry about. Just a wrong number."

Charles flipped the front burner onto high. He diced some mushrooms to get them started before cracking in two eggs. But first he wanted to see that tight nichrome coil glow bright blazing orange. Damn thing never got orange enough for him—more of a burnt apricot shade—but it radiated danger. And he found it mesmerizing.

Lately Charles was noticing that he'd become more and more interested in fire. For example, that new building under construction down by the river that was blocking everybody's view—wouldn't it be a shame if that stack of plywood was to go up in a glorious symphony of five-alarm flames? Where's Stephen King's wicked little fire-starter when you need her? A competent psychologist might have warned that this obsession suggested a metaphor for the inferno that consumed most of the oxygen that might otherwise nourish his brain. But screw those head-shrinking ass-wipes. What do they know? They'd probably try to draw some weird connection between the actual welding blowtorch that Charles kept in his trunk and the symbolic embers that smoldered in his soul.

Chapter 5

In addition to everything else, getting fired had really disrupted his routine, and free time was not something Charles was particularly good at optimizing. He could start looking for jobs tomorrow. Or the next day. Today felt like a good day to just relax, read the paper, watch some TV and do a little writing.

The problem with reading newspapers and watching TV was that it tended to just piss him off. Sure, the paper always had a sprinkling of lighter fare amid the dark, daily accounting of the never-ending nastiness—like, a feature story about some local kid who made it to age eighteen without getting molested or shot—but never enough to make the world seem like an OK place. Plus, his deteriorating vision had made his squinty attempts to read newsprint another escalating source of ire. What kind of an omniscient god gives his miraculous creations a body whose circulatory, respiratory, and central nervous systems are capable of lasting 75, even 100 years, but whose eyeballs start going bad before you even hit 50?

Still, he couldn't help himself. Charles was addicted to crime news. It confirmed his conviction that the world is a cruel, hateful place. Today it was the latest follow-up on that cop who befriended a senile old lady shortly before her death, did a few nice deeds for her, all so he could worm his way into her will... to the tune of $2.6 million. Thank goodness her original beneficiaries were determined to see justice—the ones who were frozen out after Officer Way Too Friendly consulted six lawyers before finding one willing to pretend the widow was competent enough to gift practically everything she owned to the dashing young policeman she met when he came to her house that night she imagined the place was surrounded by shadowy burglars.

It sounded like the thirty-something cop outright wooed the ninety-something widow, doing his part to feed her hallucinations that they were in love. Even if his scam did not break any laws (and there was mounting evidence that it most certainly did)—how the hell does a law enforcement professional make the moral calculation that he is entitled to inherit millions from an enfeebled elderly woman he had only known for several months? To serve and collect. The dirty cop's superiors failed to put a stop to it. Now the whole mess was headed to court.

Charles was imagining the sound of a pounding gavel, a courtroom scene in which a jury finds the cop guilty of being a soulless scumbag and sentences him to not less than 3-6 years in the state penitentiary. There he envisioned the prison gangs all ganging up on him (because they all love their mothers and grandmothers!) for a cellblock beat-down that (leaving out the lurid details in favor of an R-rated version) would likely involve a flurry of boots and tattooed fists, a creative arsenal of homemade blunt instruments and a blubbering ex-cop soiling his prison-issue skivvies.

So yes, reading the newspaper was always iffy. And when it came to in-your-face reminders about the depths of human depravity, television was definitely no better. But what the heck. He clicked on the tube. *"Family of unarmed black motorist killed by police on Main Street wants answers..."*

He began to seethe. Charles felt like his faulty wiring put him at high risk of hating just about anybody—rapists, racists, white supremacists, bad cops, pampered pro athletes, polo shirt tools who drape sweaters over their shoulders, school shooters, gun nuts who let children fire automatic weapons, Wall Street dicks, dirt bags who beat their women, most politicians, the corporate overlords who bought his newspaper and got him canned, much of humankind in general. But the depraved lunatics who were soiling his country today often made his head feel like it was three seconds away from turning into a mushroom cloud.

As someone who considered himself rational, he could think of at least one reason why a lot of people voted for the "Grab 'em by the pussy" guy. The country's power structure was way out of whack and maybe they figured it was a good idea to send in a charismatic blowhard to tear down the whole thing from the inside. But that plan blew up in everybody's face like an Acme atomic bomb.

Chapter 6

Dear Me...

Charles had begun journaling lately—part of a renewed effort to actually get started on the book he'd been involuntarily "writing" in his head since age nine. He had a profound curiosity about his descent into whatever increasingly bizarre state of mind he was descending into, and he'd discovered that the writing revealed some insight and even felt mildly cathartic.

He had long ago ruled out the idea of consulting a mental health professional, figuring that doing so would likely lead to involuntary commitment to an insane asylum. But that hadn't stopped him from researching the most appealing such facilities located within the continental United States, and even several abroad, to get a sense for what kind of amenities they offered—just in case.

There was McLean, of course, in Belmont, Massachusetts, known for its affiliation with Harvard, and for such high-profile patients as "Beautiful Mind" math wizard John Nash, poet Sylvia Plath and the writer David Foster Wallace. The photographs on the website looked appropriately pastoral and non-threatening, especially the one of the smiling man with the clipboard and pen seated next (too close?) to the smiling short-haired woman in black cradling with both hands a cup that they wanted you to believe contained tea or coffee, but that could have been spiked with any number of toxic substances. Its mission statement claimed that the facility specialized in "conducting state-of-the art scientific investigation to maximize discovery and accelerate translation of findings toward achieving prevention and cures."

"Prevention" sounded good, especially since Charles was acutely aware that he spent a considerable portion of each day trying to prevent unfortunate things from happening. And "state-of-the art scientific investigation" certainly resonated with his sense of himself as a curious-minded soul—one whose imaginary academic achievements included earning an Ivy League quadruple Ph.D. in algebraic psychology, political photosynthesis, forensic theology and Euclidean geothermal metaphysics. So McLean was definitely high on the hypothetical list of places that might provide some measure of solace, though certainly not outright hope, should his path continue to progress in the direction he anticipated with disquisitive foreboding if not outright dread.

Why, they might even award a place of honor to a man of his caliber—one whose unceasing intellectual inquiries into his own condition surely placed him in the 99th percentile of high-functioning "wackos." Charles also liked many of the names that appeared on their staff list: Blaise Aguirre, Yanaira Alonso-Caraballo, Ross J. Baldessarini and Sabina Berretta, Ying Cao and Young Cha. And that was just A-C. Perhaps tomorrow he would examine the D-F listings.

But, like any competent-minded consumer, he felt compelled to perform his due diligence and at the very least consult the U.S. News & World Report rankings of the top U.S. medical facilities specializing in psychiatry. All subjective, of course, but McLean ranked second behind Johns Hopkins, which earned major points for making him think of "The Silence of the Lambs" and Anthony Hopkins' Oscar-winning performance as the deliciously malevolent serial killer.

He also did not rule out the Mayo Clinic (Mayo may or may not meet criteria for psychiatric needs, but definitely good for tension-easing condiment comedy). However, most of the others on the list got a hard no:

- Mass General (name too militaristic)
- New York-Presbyterian (too religious sounding)
- The Menninger Clinic in Houston (too Texas)
- Sheppard and Enoch Pratt Hospital in Baltimore (love the name Enoch, not crazy about Pratt).
- Resnick Neuropsychiatric Hospital at UCLA (yes, bonus points for any facility with "Neuro" in its name)

Alright, forget it, he told himself. All this hypothetical loony bin research was distracting his focus from the day's writing.

Dear Me...

Fought off the urge to punch a man in the face for the 12th straight day.

It wasn't just that he threw the cigarette butt on the ground with no concern whatsoever for the environment, or any awareness that his vile disregard might offend those among us who believe it is wrong, even criminal, for some 1.1 billion human smokers to collectively discard an estimated 4.5 trillion biohazardous butts onto the world's sidewalks, flower gardens, byways and beaches (beaches, for chrissake!).

It was the smug look on his "smoking is so cool" face and the aloofness with which he flicked his toxins onto our shared terra firma that repulsed me sufficiently to want to scrape out the inside of a cigarette ingredient mixing vat, shackle him to a custom-designed torture chair, yank his head back and dump down his throat and into his lungs two or three gallons of noxious blackish-gray sludge comprised of tar, ammonia, arsenic, benzene, butane, carbon monoxide, cadmium, argon, cyanide, DDT, lead, formaldehyde, various insecticides, naphthalene, methyl isocyanate from Bhopal, polonium, graphite, guar gum, rock salt, 12 different acids, high fructose corn syrup, myrrh extract and Chinese hydroxychloroquine.

Instead, I had to settle for devoutly praying to the Marlboro Man in the Sky that this air-polluting, earth-despoiling bastard will die of inoperable face cancer following a brief, intensely uncomfortable course of chemotherapy that causes his respiratory system to shrivel and his hair to fall out—before he kills untold innocent bystanders by spewing his noxious, hateful second-hand nerve gas into our atmosphere.

Fuck that asshole.

Also, Mom's birthday was today. I love her so much that it makes me want to cry.

Chapter 7

Charles clasped his hands tightly together as he walked toward the post office, squeezing hard and releasing to create a pumping effect—something like a white-knuckled, human heart, pulsating right there at the end of his sleeves.

Even though he didn't know her name, somehow the adorable, age-appropriate blonde woman behind the counter made him feel for a just moment as if the world was not just a surrealistic hellhole populated by egomaniacs, predators and scoundrels. But what he found most remarkable about her was her ability to summon just the right words for dealing with even the most challenging customer. Once while pretending to write his return address on a large manila envelope, he had watched her deflect a crude come-on from a slovenly middle-aged Lothario wearing a navy blue NY baseball cap, saying, "Where I come from, gentlemen have the decency to treat a woman with a good deal more respect." The smirk melted from his face and the man's shoulders slumped as he slunk away from the counter.

Zing! Zap! Ouch! She just destroyed you. Now get the hell out of her post office, you Yankee-loving dickhead. Despite his gloating, Charles was certain not to make eye contact as the emasculated Casanova skulked toward the door. Damn, she was good.

"Hi, my name's Charles. Charles Smith." No. *"Hello, may I trouble you for a book of Forever stamps? Perhaps something with a heart."* Um, no. Whatever. Can't hurt to practice. When he reached the door, he paused for a solid five seconds to hold it open for a woman behind him carrying a yoga mat and a Starbucks cup. Naturally, she failed to acknowledge him, but he didn't even care. Before going around the corner to his P.O. box, he cast a timid glance toward the counter.

Yes, his age-appropriate postal worker was there. She appeared to be conducting some sort of transaction with a well-dressed businessman. Charles pretended to browse a display of cards and envelopes so he could ease closer in hopes of eavesdropping on the exchange. Then she gave a soft laugh to something the man said. Suddenly, any thoughts he had entertained about trying to say words to her were now swirled up in a cloud of nervousness, paranoia and panic. He unlocked his box, grabbed the contents and got the hell out of there.

Desperate to reconnect with Stan, Charles poked his head into Mugsy's and was rewarded with one of the loudest most profane greetings he'd ever received. He bought his friend a bourbon and then fell oddly silent until Stan prodded, "What's on your mind, Charlie?" and he spilled the beans about Keri Ann. "So what's the deal, lover boy? You gonna go see your girlfriend again tomorrow?"

Yes, he planned to stop by the post office to check his mail, maybe even summon up the courage to buy some stamps. But no, he certainly didn't think of the errand as "going to see his girlfriend." If he did, he would no doubt chicken out.

Charles knew his friend was teasing him about his curiosity in a member of the opposite sex, and he was determined not to take the bait. In fact, he was trying not to think about her too much because, well, her not knowing that he existed obviously just seemed way safer for everybody. Better for her to have no awareness of him whatsoever than for her to look into his soul and hate what she sees. Unfortunately, his considerable capacity for denial was already being strained by the realization that his infatuation was growing stronger. But Charles felt that, where he was concerned, the term "hopeless romantic" was heartbreakingly literal—as in pointless, tragic, ill-fated and doomed.

"I think Charlie's got a crush." Dammit, just the mention of it was enough to make him blush. "Yeah," said Stan. "I thought so. Women..." Charles gritted his teeth and winced, expecting Stan to riff his own vulgar twist on the old cliché. Probably something outrageously misogynistic like, "Can't live with 'em; can't chain 'em up in the basement and make 'em your sex slave." But instead he leaned in, locked eyes with Charles and said, "I've known a few of 'em. But I'll damn sure never figure 'em out. And believe me, buddy, I've tried."

Stan paused and sipped his whiskey. "Love is rough, Charlie. Got some regrets in that department. Sweethearts I wished I'd treated better. Believe it or not, I used to be kind of an asshole," he laughed, then turned serious again. "I've taken punches from some pretty big men, but that ain't nothing next to the pain a woman can put in your heart. What about you, Charlie?"

Charles had been bracing himself for the conversation to creep into that deeply uncomfortable terrain. He'd fallen in love only once. Still thought about her way too often. Pictured her sitting next to him in the car, her sandy blonde tresses catching sunlight as she gazed at him through serene blue eyes, now moist with tears, and told him it was over. A beautiful, empathetic soul, she had tried to make it work even after she realized what she was dealing with—a shy, introspective boyfriend who seemed to have a kind heart but who definitely had a head full of demons. It hurt to think about it, so he stopped. "I could tell you, Stan. But then I'd have to... fuck you." Stan spit out his beer as he erupted with laughter.

Charles was shocked by what he had just said. Out loud. He considered himself more of an intellectual humorist, and he was relieved that Stan—now milking the moment by theatrically convulsing and smacking his hand on the bar—was so thoroughly enjoying his joke. "Wow, buddy. You're full of surprises!"

Charles smiled as he got up to hit the can. When he returned, Stan had pulled up his black "Harleys are Like Sex, the Louder the Better" T-shirt and was staring at a tattoo above his left hip. "Justine." Then he looked up and was silent for a minute before saying, in a voice much softer than what Charles was used to hearing, "I thought I might get this changed to say 'Just Me'—something like that. What do you think?" Charles just nodded.

A few drinks later, Johnny Cash started busting out "Folsom Prison Blues" over the tavern's rinky-dink sound system. Stan closed his eyes, brought his right hand to his heart, grabbed his shirt and started singing along. Rough but good.

"That there is 'Folsom Prison Blues'."

Charles had strong feelings about Johnny Cash and he dreaded hearing the song he feared might come next—the one about a boy and his father. Sure enough. Stan kept singing. Now he was strumming an invisible guitar.

"Man, I love Johnny Cash. 'Boy named Sue'!" Stan yelled. "You know it?"

Please stop. Charles' arms were locked at his sides, fists clenched. He was sweating as Stan and Johnny neared the end of their duet. He leaned down, burying his face in both hands.

"What's the matter, man. You got a problem with Johnny Cash? My voice ain't that bad, is it?"

He hadn't planned to tell Stan about his middle name. About his father. About his secrets. About his pain.

"I… love Johnny Cash for the way he turns darkness into art. But, long story, see my dad was kind of an asshole and…" Now Charles' head was ringing with yet another Johnny Cash song, "Ring of Fire."

"My father liked Johnny Cash, too," he began slowly. "Thought it'd be great fun to name his son something that would haunt him his whole life. But really, he did it because he hated me. Showed me that every day. Every way he could think of. I would have gladly taken Sue over what that son of a bitch gave me." Charles M. Smith paused, closed his eyes and drew a deep breath through his nose.

"My father. Richard Smith. Named me. Charles. Manson. Smith."

Stan was silent, eyes wide. Finally, he power-whispered, "Charles. Manson. Smith. Are you fucking kidding me? That is some pretty twisted shit."

Stan started firing off questions, but Charles was mute. His eyes looked past or through his friend, no longer transmitting ocular input to a brain that was now in another place and time.

"Stan. I gotta go… write some shit down."

Chapter 8

OK, this is long overdue, Charles thought as he kicked off his sneakers and lowered his lanky frame into the desk chair to channel his truth—back rigid, mind reeling. It was dark outside and he could hear a police siren wailing in the distance. At first, he just stared at the laptop, blanking on how to begin. But then… think of it as a fiction story, he told himself, loosely based on the life of a psychologically damaged lunatic. He started hitting keys.

The boy knew he had anger issues long before people started whispering behind his back that he might have anger issues. Anger issues? He'd been a 5-year-old anger prodigy, thanks to daily advanced training under the hard-hitting open and closed hand of the master. Thick black eyebrows and a short, white-hot fuse, his father was a free-flowing wellspring of fury. But the son had long ago mastered a certain ability to suppress, repress, grimace and go with it—lest he invite even more beatings or, worse, lose it and harm somebody else.

The boy had endured ringing words of derision covering every aspect of his existence, from his revolting physical appearance, insubordinate behavior and alleged but grossly misdiagnosed stupidity to his general worthlessness and his deeply resented, unplanned origins. And his father underscored these intensely vocalized themes with a punishing regimen of physical violence.

Cruel fate for a bright, sensitive child with an innate understanding of most everything, to be forced not only to endure the profound physical and verbal abuse itself and to suffer the inevitable long-term emotional wreckage, but also to be cursed with an acute awareness of how deeply his father's psychopathy was warping his mind, manifesting as an involuntarily compulsion to deconstruct his own ongoing descent into madness.

The boy understood that, where the best parents feel an instinct to blanket their offspring in unconditional love, his father seemed driven to smother his first-born in a quilt of unreconstructed rage. The older man—stocky build, blocky jaw and itchy trigger fists—was not intelligent enough to understand that he was infecting his son's psyche with the seeds of lifelong internal conflict. But if he had been, he would not have cared; the result was the same.

Charles had been locked in a dangerous battle

with his own consciousness for as long as he could remember and it gnawed at his gut and his head—every single day. Though he yearned to lash back at his father, his self-preservation instincts forced him to compartmentalize—to forge himself into a self-styled stoic whose only tantrums were inner tantrums, whose cries and shouts would be heard by no one, except himself. At first, there had been a few muscle spasms. Tear-filled shouts of "I hate you!" that predictably fueled even greater abuse. But soon his communication methodology adhered to the strict protocol of a pragmatic survivalist. Vent your rage on the inside, violently but silently, while restricting audible vocal output almost exclusively to "Yes, sir."

And as the years passed, he came to believe that his survival depended on his ability to control these impulses, this part of himself that he hated and could not understand. But a deep sense of dread always loomed. Rarely, he would loosen his grip, and the result was never good. Once while sitting in a creative writing class in high school, he was seized by a burst of inspiration—his mind revealing what felt like the most exciting idea he had ever conceived. He grabbed his pen and began to scribble. "What if..."

When the ink stopped flowing and the faulty pen began to etch a deep white groove into the paper, he felt his anger rise. He tapped the pen, tried to make a doodle in the upper left corner to get the ink flowing. Again. Harder. In seconds he was shredding the paper with the useless pen. The idea was gone. A fire raging in its place. As it erupted, he rose from his desk and released a guttural scream. He whipped the pen onto the floor and it ricocheted back up and nicked a boy in the cheek, producing a teardrop of blood under his left eye.

Principal's office. Detention. A serious talk with his parents. A suggestion that maybe the boy should "see someone." Maybe get a prescription. Never did. Back then, he thought it actually might be fun to talk to a therapist. Knowing that his sense of mischief took a bit of the edge off the ever-present darkness, he imagined torturing some trained professional with the wild truths he could share while kicking back on that couch if his folks ever sent him to a shrink.

Instead, he would clench it all inside. Grind his teeth, bite his tongue and seethe. The boy regarded his future with dread. So, it's not as if he didn't see any of this coming.

In fact, much of it would be foretold in what some would later jokingly call his "manifesto." Writing he undertook as one of his many strategies to stay just on this side of that fine, trembling line between grievance and insanity.

Chapter 9

"Hey mister, my dad says you're a weirdo."

Yes, how adorable. A group of neighborhood kids had been taunting him for several weeks, ever since they watched him step in some dog shit—just outside the nearby dog park—and practically lose his mind. Barking some insanity about a "worthless, ass-licking mongrel... hunt you down... kick the shit out of your miserable, flea-ridden carcass... use my ill-equipped human front paws to bury you like a fucking bone!"

He didn't mean any of it, of course. He'd always thought of himself as more of a cat person, but he also loved dogs. So, definitely not his finest hour in terms of breaking with policy and accidentally allowing a public glimpse into his inner torment, but in retrospect, he was not displeased with the rhetorical flourishes invoked and the manic intensity of the delivery. He had achieved some level of the artistic in his elocution this time. And in his defense, it had been the third time in, like, a month and a half that he'd stepped in it, and he was beginning to suspect some sort of canine-human conspiracy.

No, Charles was not opposed to voicing one of his obscene, psychotic tirades out loud, but only if he believed there was no one around to hear him. In fact, he viewed the occasional solitary thunderburst as a necessary catharsis—even an essential component in his multi-pronged strategy to maintain a veneer of sanity. But this usually occurred in the sanctuary of his home. For example, when his internet connection became patchy or failed outright for even a modest period of time, he was liable to leap from his chair and spew forth a high-decibel torrent of language so blue that it would make a longshoreman turn red.

Did that make a "weirdo"? He happened to know that the kid's dad, a dickhead insurance salesman, had a man cave lined with framed photographs of *The Partridge Family*, *Gilligan's Island* and *The Munsters*. So maybe we're all a little weird. Walking over to check his mailbox he said, "Shouldn't you be in school?"

"It's Saturday, weirdo."

These kids—they were probably 12 or 13—had already broken into his car for quarters, toilet-papered his house at Halloween (and also Thanksgiving for some reason) and delivered the obligatory flaming bag of crap to his doorstep. They had even fashioned a flyer featuring a picture of Charles and the words "Beware: Homo gay sex offender psycho lives on this street," and distributed them all over the neighborhood. Charles had found one—next to posters for a Battle of the Bands and a missing beagle—staple-gunned to a telephone poll about 50 yards from his house. He understood what it was like to be young and hateful, and felt a little bit concerned for their safety. He grabbed a pile of mostly junk from his mailbox and went inside.

"Jury duty?"

Sure enough, the official letter—technically, it was a summons—looked pretty damn serious. He was being ordered to show up at the Warren B. Rudman Federal Courthouse three weeks from now and, though the summons did not specify, he suspected non-compliance would be federally "frowned upon." He certainly did not relish the thought of getting up at 6:30 a.m. to drive to Concord. But the truth, the whole truth and nothing but the truth was that he was also a little excited about sifting through clues and maybe dishing out a double-life sentence to some three-time loser.

The paperwork said he needed to confirm his participation and there was some fine print about whether there was any circumstance or hardship that might prevent him from performing his civic duty. He decided to throw himself upon the mercy of the court and dash off a quick letter to get those wheels of justice rolling.

Dear Jury Administrator—

I have received my summons to jury duty and am writing to confirm my participation. As a former journalist, I feel it is important to offer complete transparency about my status as a potential juror. Therefore, in the interest of full disclosure, I am compelled to testify that I harbor extreme prejudice against morons—ignorant, selfish people who can barely make it through life without messing things up for others. If selected as a juror, these jerks will feel my full judicial wrath. White-collar criminals will not like me either. I will try not to make an example of them by holding them personally responsible for the losses I and millions of others incurred during the meltdown of 2008. But I cannot offer any guarantees.

If the case has anything to do with New Hampshire's version of the Stand Your Ground law, I am liable to go off half-cocked. In fact, if my case has anything to do with firearms whatsoever, the jury selection experts might want to review some of my past writings—including my infamous Professor Gunn column, which prompted firearms boosters to give me a verbal blasting with both barrels. And if the case involves some scumbag whose negligence is responsible for a child shooting themselves or getting shot, the defense attorney can save his excuses. Death penalty.

If it pleases the court, here are a few other things the jury selection folks will definitely want to know about me: I detest unsubstantiated allegations. An attorney is much more likely to hold my attention if they sprinkle their oral arguments with terms like "Exhibit A," "habeas corpus" and "malfeasance."

When in a courthouse, I am sometimes overwhelmed by an involuntary urge to sue various parties, my specialty being frivolous class-action litigation with arbitrary and capricious demands for seven-figure punitive damages. I am also available to help with courtroom security, as I make it a practice to carry on my person at all times a small penknife with a laser pointer.

Thank you for considering me. I look forward to helping you lock up some sociopathic miscreants. I mean, "alleged sociopathic miscreants." Having disclosed all of my potential conflicts, predispositions and judicial eccentricities in the sworn testimony above, I stand ready to perform my civic duty as a proud citizen of the state of New Hampshire and the United States of America!"

About a week later, a pair of federal agents would appear at his door.

Chapter 10

"Jury duty, eh? I got called for jury duty once, but they ended up rejecting me due to various, shall we say, 'incidents' that showed up on my record."

Stan's laugh sounded even louder inside the cab of his raggedy, reddish-brown 1976 F-series pickup. Charles had been thrilled when Stan called to see if he wanted to help him haul a truckload of construction debris to the town dump. Charles eyeballed the truck's spartan cockpit. Dashboard thick with dust and unidentifiable substances. The sticky upholstery a mosaic of missing chunks, burn holes and lacerations. Small portholes down by his feet offered a vertigo-inducing view of the pavement.

"She's a classic, isn't she? Bought her for 75 bucks from a guy who was going away for a while. I used to think I'd restore her. But it's more fun to just keep her barely alive as I beat her ass into the ground." Stan popped Steppenwolf's "Born to Be Wild" into the 8-track and began bobbing his head. He started singing and nodded at Charles to chime in. "Awwww yeeaahh!" Stan laughed and shouted at the vaguely musical croaking sounds that came out of Charles' mouth.

They pulled into the Department of Public Works Recycling Center—better known as the dump—rolled up to the giant bin marked "Wood," hopped out and began chucking their cargo. It felt good to be doing something physical and Charles found himself enjoying the breezy air—tinged as it was with a unique potpourri of deciduous yard waste, industrial solvents and battery acid.

As Charles hurled a heavy palette, a bent rusty nail hooked on his sleeve, yanking him almost into the bin and carving a small notch through the skin near his wrist. The anger flushed his temples with rapid-response rage. And as it surged Charles fought back the urge to light up the DPW yard with one of his signature foul-mouthed screeds. *Moron!! You can't even throw a hunk of wood into a dumpster without fucking yourself in the dumper! Aaahhhhh!* His entire upper body felt tight. He wondered if it was possible to choke on the suffocating ferocity of one's own self-loathing.

"Damn, Charlie. What's goin' on in that head of yours. You look like you're about to blow a gasket, brother. You want a brew?" Stan reached into the truck and pulled a Milwaukee's Best from behind his seat. Charles shook his head. "Alright, but go easy, buddy. You don't wanna pop a fucking aneurysm."

Stan's aneurysm crack had actually started to make Charles a little paranoid. A mind as messed up as his was at high risk of full-blown hypochondria. Ever-curious about his own neuroses and psychoses, Charles fancied himself a lifelong student of the human mind and body. And his passion for research had afforded him particular insight into his own mental and medical condition. While it was true that he believed himself to be suffering from a rare combination of ADHD, PTSD and Low T, he was equally certain that no one or two or three or four diagnoses could fully express the derangement that consumed his soul. He definitely wrestled with antisocial personality disorder. Year-round seasonal affective disorder, too. And of course, schizophrenia, schizophrenia, schizophrenia.

Surely, he was afflicted with one or more ailments on the autism spectrum, or prism as he liked to think of it, most likely some exotic offshoot of Asperger's. He also grappled with bouts of agoraphobia, especially on Thursdays. He exhibited a manic interest in depression and considered himself a textbook case of repressed hyperverbalism. There was also his ongoing battle with whatever strain of obsessive-compulsive Tourette Syndrome ravaged his frenzied, yet fragile inner world.

"You still with me, Charlie?" Stan was turning onto Route 1B to take the scenic route past the grand Wentworth Hotel, Fort Constitution and the Portsmouth Naval Shipyard—Charles' favorite bicycling route. "All recovered from your trauma. Ticker still tickin' away?" Stan flutter-tapped his own heart seven times. "How 'bout your johnson?" he asked, offering a triple pelvic thrust and a gust of laughter. "Yeah, Stan. Sorry. I guess I'm just a little distracted. Crazy week."

By the time Stan dropped him off, Charles was still thinking about his heart, especially now that his employer-provided health insurance was on life support. Surely he was at low risk for myocardial infarction, pulmonary embolism or deep vein thrombosis. And, at age fifty-three, he was a little too young to get overwrought about possible atrioventricular fistula or nonbacterial thrombotic endocarditis. Then again, he did occasionally experience dizziness, weakness and fatigue. And some of his epic tirades were known to induce a vague sense of cerebrovascular discomfort. An EKG was out of the question due to his lifelong aversion to electrodes. But perhaps just to be safe he should have himself checked out for elevated blood levels of asymmetric dimethylarginine.

Not surprisingly, his habit of obsessing about all the actual maladies triggered that mechanism in his cerebral cortex that prompted him to involuntarily concoct imaginary ones as well. Call it the old "diffuse fear of mortality with humor" reflex. Different hemorrhagic strokes for different folks. Seriously, one can never take too many precautions to guard against the ever-present risk of varicose brain, cerebral hemorrhoids and fudge sickle cell anemia. Not to mention curvature of the liver, metaphysical vomitosis and unmitigated gallstones. Studies have shown side effects of such unchecked medical ribaldry may include degenerative pharmaceutical-industrial complex, congressional meningitis, soul weevils, and chronic bubonic plague. Fortunately, new research indicates that people who consume 50 milligrams of cornpone each day are

32 percent less likely to suffer from rickets, rabies and shingles.

Sexually speaking, he had long ago self-diagnosed himself as suffering from Gender Nonspecific Penile Dissociative Syndrome. But that was just the tip of the iceberg. He suspected his capacity for intimacy also was hobbled by restless hand syndrome and post-orgasmic stress disorder. And that his adult-onset celibacy was likely exacerbated by penile sclerosis and low pud pressure. Meanwhile, that surgeon general guy was always reminding him that life as we know it may be hazardous to your health. Exhausted, Charles took two aspirin, three Vitamin C, five Tums, a couple globules of Omega-3 fish oil, then passed out on the couch.

Chapter 11

Knock, knock, knock.

Charles opened the door to find two close-cropped, dark-suited strangers. "Are you Charles Manson…" he glanced down at a notebook in his left hand, "Smith?"

Damn right I am, you jack-booted government goons.

Shh. "Who's asking, please?"

"Special Agent Phillips," said Goon No. 1, who then nodded to his partner, "and Special Agent Winchester. We'd like to come inside and speak with you for a moment." As he stepped back to let the two men in, Charles resolved to limit his word count during the encounter to no more than 20.

"Well Mr. Smith, it seems your unusual response to the jury duty summons caused a little bit of a red flag situation. So we got orders to pay you a visit and assess your mental well-being, just to make sure you don't pose a threat to the public… or to yourself."

"Thank you, gentlemen." (Word tally: 3.)

"So what's the deal, Mr. Funny Guy? When people start

making noise about going off half-cocked and bringing knives and lasers into a federal courtroom, we start to get a little curious. Understand?" Charles nodded. He had no immediate plans to do anything drastic. Worst case, he was pre-postal and he doubted there was any precedent for suicide by self-induced aneurysm.

"See, we went ahead and read some of that crap you used to write in the newspaper, Professor Gunn. No wonder you got blasted in the comments section. You were asking for it." The agent looked at his notebook again to quote some of Charles' own words back to him. The dark, satirical piece took the form of a fake advice column with letters to a fictional firearms expert, Professor Gunn.

"Dear Professor Gunn—I'm kind of a ticking time bomb. I've got more guns than I know what to do with. I'm super anti-social, and I often feel confused and depressed. Plus, I keep hearing about these party poopers who want to limit the number of bullets I can fire without reloading my so-called assault rifles. That sure would stink for a guy like me."

The agent shook his head and looked back up at Charles. "Perhaps you can see why we might be a little concerned."

Most assuredly, you power-tripping pinhead, Charles thought, *I assume it is predominantly due to an inability to wrap your pea brain around the time-honored concept of satire.* Charles squinted at him. "Sir?" (Running word tally: 4.)

"It's just that, our experience has shown that a guy like you is potentially way more dangerous than some run-of-the-mill gun nut." He peered down at his notebook again.

"And this article with your name on it—'Value the Human Race Over the Arms Race.' Here you suggest that in heaven there would be, quote, 'no Bushmaster assault rifles (main purpose: slaughtering human beings). No .22s, .45s or AK-47s. No submachine guns or semi-automatics. No Derringers, Gatlings or Colts. No howitzers, bazookas or Uzis. No rocket launchers or M-16s. No Saturday-night specials or Sunday go-to-meetin' Magnums.' End quote. Pretty subversive shit, if you ask me."

Thank you for acknowledging my work. I've got something else for you to read. It's called the First Amendment, bitches. Charles wished he had the guts to say as he examined the agent's waistband and his torso, wondering how many guns he might be carrying and how quickly the man could whip one out and empty its chamber into his chest. "Just words in a newspaper, sir." (Running word tally: 10)

"OK, buddy. But you might consider being a little more careful about what you write. Because we don't want to have to come back here again. *Comprende?*"

Sí, comprende, Tony Montana. What next, you cock-a-roach? I gotta say hello to your little friend? Pause. "Yes, sir. I apologize for wasting your valuable time." (Final word tally: 19.)

As the agents began walking back to their black SUV, Charles felt his irritation rising. *"Hey assholes!"* he did not shout. One of the men turned. He made a peace sign and pointed it at his eyes, then pointed the two fingers at Charles, who could not help but smirk. "Buh-bye," Charles whispered to himself.

About a half-hour later, he went outside to check the mail.

"Freeze! FBI!"

Charles went cold and thrust his hands toward the sky.

"Ha-ha. Ha-ha-ha!"

The three boys ran past him, laughing at their joke—mocking the jittery, middle-aged neighbor, playfully preying on his predilection for nightmarish daydreams. The ringleader whirled around and flipped him the bird. Then he tossed his skateboard out ahead into the street, jumped on and gave a few pumps with his right leg as his two hench-punks followed.

There might be some hope for the other two, but that ringleader was trouble. He regularly prowled the neighborhood with his slingshot and BB gun, hunting squirrels and birds. And Charles couldn't recall ever observing such sneering contempt in a face that young. He'd rung the doorbell at the boy's house to alert his parents to the fake sex offender poster, but the dad just brushed him off. The fact that he practically laughed in his face suggested he was impressed by junior's handiwork.

So we like pranks do we, little scamps? Well, old Charles has been known to pull a prank or two in his day. His mind flashed through a scrapbook of unsettling images: A baby doll swinging from a makeshift noose; his brother's bed crawling with crayfish; his own younger self splayed lifeless on the kitchen floor, novelty "vampire blood" oozing from his eyes and mouth as his mother screamed; his father glaring at him, a wisp of smoke rising from an exploded cigarette that dangled from his lips. A man in an EMT uniform performing emergency medical treatment on a lifeless form lying in the street. (Wait, what?)

Chapter 12

Charles had decided that writing counted as a legitimate, even therapeutic form of procrastination from searching for a new job. He'd also begun jokingly thinking of his laptop rantings as a "manifesto."

Heard the song "Mellow Yellow" on the radio today. Something about it made me feel a little less like embarking on a murderous rampage to avenge all the wrongs being perpetrated on those less fortunate by corrupt, greedy fucks in positions of power. Just kidding, sort of. I had to watch two AC/DC videos ("Jailbreak" and Hell's Bells") just to re-establish my equilibrium.

Anyway, dreading the job search. Not feeling motivated. Not sure what to do. Even if I get lucky and land another newspaper job, who's to say I don't just get laid off again six months down the road? Maybe I should apply at the post office. Plus, Stan said he might have an opportunity for me. Eager to hear more about that. I don't even know what he does. Scary SOB, but hanging out with him makes me feel almost good.

A car alarm rang out, causing Elmer to scramble from his cushioned resting spot in the living room bay window. Charles begun to feel like a tea kettle about to blow, his internal steam valves shrieking in time with the unseen automotive nuisance. God, he hated car alarms and how they provoked thoughts of sledgehammers and shattered windshields. He wouldn't literally fire a gun at it if he had one, but thinking about it seemed to help. Part of him wanted to kill the inventors and manufacturers of car alarms. Not literally kill them, of course, but maybe just station outside each of their houses a device that played the car alarm sound, perhaps mixing in a skip-riddled, high-decibel loop of Van Halen's "Panama" or other songs said to be popular among psychological warfare DJs. Surely these car alarm jerks knew that, if their wretched devices had ever prevented the theft of a single automobile, which he doubted, they had caused far more aggravation to millions of people. He looked outside, but it was too dark to see anything. Finally, the hate-honking stopped.

Fingers hovering above the keyboard, he tried to focus on sitting up straight for more than fifteen seconds. But it just wasn't going to happen. His posture sucked, but the car alarm had left his mind juiced like a live wire knocked loose in a storm. Synapses popping with sparks and snapping sounds. Cranial chemicals burning bright colors.

Lighting a path into dark places in his head that most days felt too horrifying to explore. It was overwhelming. But the high-voltage buzz of mental adrenaline propelled him forward. And he began to write.

Charles never looked back at the explosion—his explosion—as flames engulfed the now-shuttered shithole where he spent most of his deeply troubled childhood.

That place was crammed to the asbestos-riddled rafters with ghosts. And though this might not kill them, it would sure as hell show them who was boss.

Tilting his head, he could hear echoes of his father, tough guy, bellowing at him, every third word starting with F, the air next to his fat face dotted with saliva. "How the fuck did I get stuck with such a fucked-up little fuckface crybaby? Can't even get through one fucking week at school without fucking things up. Next time you want to shove a fucking crayon in some kid's mouth, picture my hand smacking your stupid fucking face, you little piece of shit. Giving the Manson family a bad name."

Yes. Bad enough Charles had to get teased for being the odd kid, the one with "behavioral issues," the one who never felt quite right in his own skin and knew the other kids could sense it. He also had to be the butt of his father's greatest joke. Richard and Clare Manson didn't even have the decency to tell their son he shared the same name as one of the most reviled figures in American history. He had to figure that one out on the playground. Thanks, pop.

"Who's daddy's little Charles Manson?" His father thought the whole thing was hilarious. Make the boy tough, like some twisted ode to his hero Johnny Cash.

The explosion, the fire—it was years in the making. The family had long since moved and the place was now broken down and abandoned, a cracked Big Wheel half-buried amid the ivy that still crept up the wall toward his old bedroom window. Charles had long fantasized about burning it down, even though he knew he couldn't cauterize a psychological wound at its geographical source. Hadn't seen the place in four or five years, but now he had made a special trip, on break between semesters.

Sitting on the stone wall staring at it, he smoked a joint to try to chill—achieve a calmer state as he looked inside to see if he had the guts to do it or if he was too much of a coward. He'd brought all the supplies a rookie arsonist would need, but he could already feel himself chickening out. Spineless jerk-off. He wondered where the old man was now. Richard Manson. Fucking Dick. Charles was 14 when his mom made her escape—hustling he and Billy into the station wagon one night and driving to the airport for a flight to California, that drunken brute slumped and snoring in his chair. He could still hear Ed McMahon laughing as they left.

She was her son's hero, and it destroyed him when she died of cancer just three years later. At least while she was still alive, there was a glimmer of light in the world. He and his brother didn't talk much anymore. Billy had problems of his own. The old man? Sitting in front of that house, Charles could see his face clearly. Then he pictured it with all the flesh rotted away, leaving only a hollow-eyed skull with a shitty comb-over. That's how he'd rather remember his father, but he could never shake the flashbacks.

He shook his head and stood up, the duffel bag with the gas can and accessories laying at his feet. He zipped his jacket, spit on his moon-lit shadow and walked down the darkened street. Head down, hands in his pockets, he understood that if he ever did summon up the courage to create such a spectacular explosion, he probably would not be walking away from it.

Holy shit, thought Charles. *What just happened?*

Experiencing a heightened sense of anxious euphoria, he put his hand to his head, pretending to check himself for a fever and imagined he could feel his heart pumping against the cotton threads of his Speed Racer T-shirt.

Charles leaned back and emerged from his own life story, names slightly altered to amplify the insanity. He felt empowered by his instinct to drop his real-life surname and explore the dramatic tension implicit in his "character" being named Charles Manson, no more Smith. Maybe he'd flip 'em and pop Smith in the middle for his tortured protagonist. Charles S. Manson!

The move felt oddly liberating—as if this fictional embrace of his "inner Manson" and the blunt impact of those four syllables might give him greater insight into his own tortured soul. There was an aspect of, "Dude, that sick fuck who gave you half of your DNA christened you Charles Manson for a reason. Own it." Of course, he didn't mean "Tattoo a swastika onto your forehead and go on a helter-skelter killing spree" own it. It was more like a "Try not to beat yourself up quite as much for being a socially challenged, thermonuclear-tempered mutant" kind of thing.

Side benefit: Renaming the father—calling him Manson—was a way of returning the favor. A way of branding him, Richard F. Smith, as evil for naming a baby after a murderous cult leader. "Yes, Manson," he mused with just a hint of a grin.

He reflected on the fact that he, Charles Manson Smith, was an internally volatile but relatively benign entity, arguably quite cowardly, in fact—verbally eviscerating the world's assholes in his mind before meekly acquiescing to their unending provocations in real life. But this Charles S. Manson character seemed like a borderline badass, ready to confront any damn thing—maybe even himself. In the book.

Chapter 13

Elmer was gazing out the bathroom window, his usual perch at this hour of the morning, knowing it would be Charles' first stop when he rolled out of bed for bodily functions and personal hygiene. (Brush teeth. Run razor over chin, cheeks and upper lip. Berate self in mirror for looking like such a fucking idiot.)

Usually he'd step on the scale—just to get a quick numerical reading on how his bipolar, body dysmorphic, binge-and-ban dietary regimen was impacting his multifaceted self-loathing on that particular day. On the spectrum of force-feeding himself a lo-carb diet to "get in shape," then abandoning all pretense of nutritional well-being to gorge his esophageal abyss of emotional and spiritual emptiness on an imbalanced diet of sweet and salty treats, 180-185 was considered "good" while anything above 185 (his record was 214) risked nudging the needle toward "hateful." It usually took him a good week or two to add several inches of flab to his midsection, but by exercising his considerable powers of self-denial he could usually drop 10 pounds in the span of several days.

"Who's my little best friend? Is it you?" He rubbed the cat's head, nuzzled his nose and continued the conversation. "Rainy out there. Did you sleep well? Any good dreams?" The cat examined him, then hopped down and scampered through the door. He liked to lead the way into the kitchen.

"You must be hungry for breakfast."

"Meow," said Elmer.

Charles was not the least bit concerned, didn't find it at all odd, that an eleven-pound, fur-covered creature who didn't speak a word of English had been his best friend for more than a decade. Actually, then or now, it was no contest. Seriously, Stan's a great guy and everything, but he's no Elmer. This cat was not into head games. He respected Charles and they shared an understanding about balancing affection and playtime with the need to give each other their space.

His cat was cool, no doubt about that. Unlimited potential. Charles could even imagine him becoming an online super-cat. Crazy? Last time he checked, the internet had elevated countless felines to international acclaim. Of course, he wondered how this might affect their friendship, whether the fame would mess with Elmer's tiny head. Charles wondered how he would handle it, too. What if his cat started earning more money than he did? Would he become resentful? He thought about stuff like this practically every day. You know, normal stuff.

Five minutes later, Charles was starting to get pissed off. His attempts to innocently stalk Keri Ann on Facebook had instead ushered in an onslaught of unwanted annoyances. He did not care that a high school acquaintance had recently bonfired two big piles of brush. He did not want to know the latest miracle secret for achieving firmer arms in just 60 seconds. And he did not "like" the picture of the stupid ham sandwich and pickle that mustard-faced idiot Jonathan Morton was having for lunch.

There was an ex-colleague's revelation that he hates Chicken McNuggets, some desperate soul's all-caps rebuke of a loved one and the latest quiz (Karen is a Peruvian spider monkey, which species of simian are you?).

And, of course, politics… on Facebook. An informed and engaged electorate discussing the vital social and political issues of our time is essential to a healthy democracy… on Facebook. Time-tested ideals of the Founding Fathers meet oxymorons… on Facebook.

Facebook was by far Charles' favorite place to virtually hate people—the politicians as well as the messed-up masses. It offered a reliably toxic political smogscape where he could find tools of disinformation spouting off about "socialism," without a flicker of comprehension about the stars and stripes being dimmed and stripped by those abusing power and privilege instead of using it for the common good.

He hated the idea of being the guy who was intolerant of opposing viewpoints, but the right's appeal to millions left him dumbstruck. Of course, Democratic politicians sucked donkey ass as well. Willpower, Charles. Don't take the bait this time. Hey look, the only woman he'd ever loved was posting prom pictures of her teenagers.

Chapter 14

"BAM! BAM! BAM! BAM! BAM! BAM! BAM!"

Jesus! Charles was wildly aware that he was prone to hyperbole when describing the people, events and objects that would never stop kicking him in the head. He understood that, acoustically speaking, the actual sound that raged forth from that goddamn nuisance in the sky was much different than the pounding it created inside his skull. But that thing was beginning to sound like a fucking jackhammer. He gritted his teeth and gazed skyward. The red helicopter looked tiny up there, as it traced a swift line toward a point directly above where he stood. He had walked down to the grassy park by the river thinking he would soothe his mind while basking in the rarified, riparian air.

Now he was conflicted. Charles liked the idea that an aeronautical entrepreneur could achieve liftoff with a new business chartering scenic midair tours of the historic oceanfront tourist mecca he called home. And yet, something about the way the rotors chopped up the engine's roar and spit it rippling into his ears like enemy submachine gun fire intensified his rising hatred of these angry passenger mosquitoes on steroids.

"You know Charlie," Stan would tell him later, "I used to fly Hueys back when I was in country. Man, what a rush. Hovering just above the tree line. Some psycho from Wyoming hanging off one of the skids with a .50-cal Browning M2 spitting rounds at the VC, howling "Die, you communist motherfuckers!" When Charles stared, waiting for more, Stan allowed a grin. "OK, I juiced up that last part a little bit. But I did fly choppers."

The helicopter passed, moving north toward Maine. Charles let out a sigh and resumed his walk. His favorite water fountain was a round brick pool with a statue standing in the center of a chiseled bronze Neptune holding a trident in his left hand while looking up at a fish he held aloft in his right. The fish spurted a high, arching stream of water.

A plaque affixed to the bricks told the story of Ensign Charles Emerson Hovey (1885–1911), a local man who served as a Navy officer during the Philippine-American War. Charles was so fascinated by the story on the plaque that he stopped to read it almost every time he visited the park. The story of this other, long-ago local Charles read: "As he commanded a detachment of men from the USS *Pampanga* in pursuit of outlaw Moros on the island of Basilan, his party was ambushed and he himself was mortally wounded." The names sounded exotic, his ultimate sacrifice heroic. Charles tossed a penny into one of the four shallow, shell-shaped basins that ringed the pedestal.

Charles admired the statue. A remarkable physical specimen, the figure looked poised, courageous and confident. It stood perfectly still, probably had for decades or longer—a calm yet commanding presence, making no sound, betraying no emotion. The very essence of stoicism. He heard a seagull squawking over by the fishing boats. In the distance, there was another sound. And goddammit it was getting louder.

"BAM! BAM! BAM! BAM! BAM!"

The noise rattled his head. He pivoted and started speed-walking toward the center of town.

"Yes, please. A large Ethiopian?" The man-bunned barista slid him a tall, hot, heavy paper cup and some coins that he jangled into the tip jar. The closest Charles ever came to what most people think of as relaxation involved sitting down to sip a coffee outside Above Average Joe in Portsmouth's brick-paved Market Square.

He loved to gnarl himself into one of those uncomfortable green, wrought-iron chairs and mind his own business while watching, and listening to, his little corner of the world roll and stroll by. Of course, he was hardly minding his own business. Here, his inclination toward self-absorbed introspection was interrupted by full-on, antennae-up eavesdropping. Surveying the scene as he dosed himself with caffeine, he soaked up data from fellow coffee-sippers and passers-by as they talked about everything from remedies for dry skin and recipes for butternut squash to why the flag is at half-staff this time—all the while knowing that the latest annoyance was never more than half a block away.

The sun warmed his face and made him squint a bit as he watched sparrows hunt and peck for pastry crumbs. An older gentleman with a laptop had his sleepy golden retriever sprawled across the tight little corridor amid the outdoor seating, as if aiming to block the maximum amount of sidewalk humanly—or caninely—possible. Beautiful dog. Neither he nor his master noticed nor cared that people were being forced to step over him. If he wasn't feeling so relaxed, Charles would have fantasized about taking an industrial-strength Flowbee to the dog owner's ridiculous page-boy haircut.

And when did they pass a law that everyone under age twenty-seven must walk through town—thumbs flittering, eyes focused on their phones, white buds and wires sprouting from their ears—using their peripheral vision not to notice anything about their surroundings, but solely to avoid bumping into them? *Wake up!* his mind yelled. These fools did not know what they were missing. Why, a well-trained ear could hear absurdist street poetry, inscrutable Zen koans in nearly every snippet of random conversation, every quirky stream of human consciousness.

Behind him, a brawny young man engaged in a church-front chat (Charles thought he may have heard mention of a flask) invited a conversation partner to guess his weight. "Two-sixty?" Nope. Four hundred. Or to be more precise, "400 pounds of fury," said he, adding for emphasis, "I'm a thoroughbred beast." To his left, Charles heard a woman with a Southern accent say, "Nobody in my family owned any slaves." Jesus, what stray thought or provocative comment could possibly illicit such a strange declaration?

Just then, a thickly built older fellow with white hair and a backpack walked up, extended his hand and said, "I wanted to apologize. I had mistaken you for somebody else..." Hmm, puzzling. "I thought you were a friend of mine," he politely explained, "when I called you a dickhead from over there." He pointed across the street toward the bus stop. "Oh, I didn't even hear you." Charles was more amused than annoyed. "So, no offense taken."

The man continued slowly, as if impaired by a state of mild intoxication or some not-quite-debilitating chemical imbalance. "Yeeaahh, so I just wanted to make my amends." OK, please go away now, Charles thought, assuring him that his *mea culpa*, though appreciated, was definitely not necessary. The man fumbled with the wording of another half-apology. Then, having sufficiently unburdened his guilt over the unheard insult, he asked if he could "borrow" a couple bucks for a slice of pizza, before disappearing down Congress Street.

Charles resumed his examination of his tiny, urban ecosystem—noticing shopping bags from cleverly named boutiques; G.Willikers! was his favorite—and musing that, for his money, the clopping hooves of the horse-drawn carriage was, hands down, the best sound in town. On the information kiosk—next to a poster for a missing white cat named Wazoo—he spied a flyer for a book launch party.

The cover of *This Is Not My Bathing Suit* featured the title printed atop a woman's bikini-clad body.

Mmmm, sex, he thought, taking a moment to mull possible cover themes for his own masterpiece. A bikini-clad woman strutting from the scene of a massive explosion. Or perhaps two of them sashaying away from an even more epic explosion, the blonde one cupping a hand next to her mouth to megaphone a catchphrase to her partner over the pandemonium. Cheesy as hell, but he thought either of these would offer far more appeal than his current concepts—a grinning monkey manipulating the strings of a tiny dancing human marionette; or a rumpled, middle-aged loser, hands covering his ears, his face contorted in an expression inspired by Edvard Munch's *The Scream*.

A sharp red helicopter droned in the distant horizon, cutting a wide loop around the scenic downtown. But before Charles could get riled up anew about those insufferable whirly-birds, a trio of motorcyclists rolled up Pleasant Street and pulled up to the curb. He knew that, by law, he must share his favorite coffee spot with the mix of legit motorcyclists and dillwad leather-clad wannabes blotting out his ability to hear odd slices and morsels of life, or much of anything at all. He appreciated that most of the riders made an effort to limit the noise pollution, but others just loved to play spin the throttle.

This group appeared to be the latter. As two more of their number rumbled up, Charles wondered whether these guys were gunning for the record for wrecked conversations with their mortar fire. Less than 12 feet away, amplified amid the echo chamber of tall brick buildings, a 90-second symphony of thunder slammed through his external auditory canal and into his tympanic membrane with the force of many thousand horsepower, rocking his vestibular and cochlear nerves, and rattling his ossicles before ripping down his eustachian tubes and blasting straight into his cranium. Now fully enraged, Charles was imagining another explosion—this one with twisted motorcycle frames and burnt-leather carcasses instead of bikini models.

Chapter 15

Charles had never doubted his ability to write an OK novel. But he also understood that in order to become a novelist, one had to actually write a goddamn novel. Now that he had finally cracked open that can of snakes and felt an unexpected—and, yes, unsettling—surge of momentum, he did not consider it presumptuous to spend a few moments thinking about who might play various key characters in the blockbuster film adaptation.

He wished Philip Seymour Hoffman was still alive. He obviously needed someone dark and edgy to play the dangerous and enigmatic Charles Manson Smith. Bryan Cranston would kill as Charles, but he was probably too busy. Robert Downey Jr. was too handsome. Actually, everybody was too handsome but that's what makeup departments are for. Nicolas Cage—too on the nose? Keanu Reeves could certainly handle the minimalist man of constant restraint character trait. Maybe Steve Buscemi.

Swaggering sixty-something Stan would be tough. Michael Keaton was the first face to pop into his mind's eye. Sean Penn? De Niro? Pacino? Harvey Keitel? He liked Scarlett Johansson for Keri Ann (*Lost in Translation*! Note to self: Find part for Bill Murray). Of course, Jennifer Lawrence absolutely crushed him in *Silver Linings Playbook*. By the end of his imaginary casting session, he had also made space on the short list for Kirsten Dunst and Reese Witherspoon.

But his maybe-someday, maybe-not novel was not going to put Friskies brand shreds in Elmer's bowl. So he shifted his attention to imagining what kind of job he might find. Best case, he figured that between his modest savings and his lavish (sarcastic for puny) severance package, he might be OK till spring, maybe even cover his ass with some Obamacare. He knew there'd be no newspaper jobs within a 50-mile radius. But he started by checking out the online listings at his old employer. The paid classifieds were once considered a cash cow for newspapers. Today there were four jobs listed. Four. He went to Monster.com and Indeed.com, examined the Help Wanteds for jobs he would never apply for and imagined reading between the lines.

Collection Specialist in Dover: Associate leg-breaker. Must have menacing physical presence and zero sympathy for liberal arts moochers who get behind on their six-figure student loans.

Surgical Scheduling Coordinator in Exeter: "Yes, Mr. Smith. I've got you down for a 10 a.m. rotator cuff job, then we'll pop in your new pacemaker at 3:45. Of course, your insurance will cover only a portion of the cost, leaving you with a bill that will bankrupt you unless you are rich."

Lawn Mowing Foreman in York: Must be able to drive a one-ton dump truck with trailer. Also must have lifelong passion for grass and be willing to wield the most ridiculous power tool ever created by man, the leaf blower.

Skin Wellness/Medical Esthetician: Must be skilled in conning lovely, intelligent women into believing they cannot make it through life without purchasing hideously expensive salves, creams, and potions marketed to prey on their insecurities about how they conform to society's impossibly unrealistic standards for female beauty.

Inside Sales Account Executive for SellMyTimeShareNow.com: $55K plus earning potential with no cap. Charles was no salesman, but he enjoyed picturing himself as Alec Baldwin in "Glengarry Glen Ross," leveraging his skill in stringing together thundering obscenities to light a fire under the asses of spineless losers.

> "What's my name? Fuck you! That's my name!"

As soon as he switched over to Craigslist, one listing leapt off the page and smacked him hard in the face. "Help wanted: Ghostwriter."

Very intriguing, but likely too good to be true. "Retired cop. Seeks ghostwriter to help with novel project. Will pay top dollar to right individual." Charles whipped up a cordial, professional response citing not only his decades of experience as a writer and editor and several long-ago journalism awards, but also his sessions as a creative writing coach in a local adult education program. He did not mention his failure to achieve his long-held goal of getting a humor piece accepted by the New Yorker. Nor did he divulge the fact that such an esteemed literary authority as his own father had once called him "the shittiest piece of shit writer in Shitsburgh," or that the spiteful testimonial cited above had inspired him, finally, to begin cranking out the Grating American Novel he had always felt destined to write.

When the man who placed the ad responded almost immediately, Charles was thrilled to learn that, though he loathed the local paper, he'd read some of his columns and didn't hate them. The man made a sly reference to one piece, joking that he, too, believed that global warming was caused by increased activity in hell.

Now, armed only with his iPad, Charles was walking to the man's house for a meeting/job interview. He was still a good 100 feet away from the ex-cop's 18th century South

End home when a canine security system began barking its ass off. Charles' right hand positioned itself in front of his groin area. Damn, this thing sounded vicious.

When Lt. Roger Quentin opened the door, he said, "Don't mind, Brutus. He just gets a little bloodthirsty if he goes longer than 24 hours without ripping into some human flesh. Joking, of course. I'm Roger Quentin and this strapping young lad is Brutus."

"Charles Smith. Thank you for seeing me." His extended right hand was met with an overly aggressive grip that he was certain was intended to send a message. Something along the lines of: "I'm used to exerting power and authority over every motherfucker I meet. So don't fuck with me, candy-ass. Cause I could just as easily smack you in the face as offer you a Fresca."

Charles squinted one eye and peered back at him as if to say: *Look doughnut hole, your Captain Badass routine doesn't scare me. I've had tougher assholes than you busting my nuts and pouring Budweiser on my fucking head since I was 4 years old.* But then Brutus nuzzled his leg and he flinched, so his end of the stare-down came off as something more like: *Jiminy Cricket, mister, keep that scary dog away from me and I'll do whatever you say.*

"Don't give me that Charles Smith bullshit, man. You're Charles MANSON Smith. I know who you are. I've done my homework. And I know what you're capable of... as a writer. That's why you're here. Shall we get down to business?" Charles nodded and Quentin led him into an impressive basement man cavern ringed with taxidermy heads—wildebeest, leopard, giraffe, pachyderm, grizzly bear and more; was that an albino black rhino and why is that chimpanzee wearing an eye patch?—each sporting a scowl more intimidating than the last. "I put that one down with a blow dart," he said, whirling and whipping out a samurai sword as he gestured to a wild-eyed Tasmanian devil.

The almost comically macho décor also included a firearms collection featuring muskets, blunderbusses and a desktop Gatling gun; a human skull with a bullet hole piercing the frontal lobe and a black velvet painting of dogs gunning each other down after a poker game gone wrong. Quentin nodded toward a chair upholstered with Cape buffalo hide, silently ordering him to sit. "Look, I'm a rich, retired cop, soldier of fortune type asshole," he said. "I've killed wild animals on five continents and alleged criminals in five countries.

"My veins are still pulsing with enough testosterone to tag Kim Kardashian, the Real Housewives of Fucking Honolulu and your mother, but my doctor says my ticker needs a breather and I have to, ummph, tone things down a bit. So for my next act, I'm looking to bang out an action-adventure-terror best-seller that makes Ernest Hemingway look like Harry Potter." Charles was not sure exactly what steroid-amphetamine combo this guy was on but nodded vigorously, sensing that failure to do so might result in a caning.

"The way this works is, I talk at you like I am right now for a couple hours a day. You write it down and make me sound even more amazing than I already am. Job pays 60 bucks an hour, 10 hours a week. What do you say?" Petrified but intrigued, Charles loosened his grip on the arms of the chair.

"You've come to the right writer, Lieutenant. We'll give 'em Sherlock Bronson meets James Wolverine Bond." He did not know what this meant either, but it seemed to satisfy the heavily armed lunatic with the savage attack dog poised by his side. "Good. We start tomorrow at 10. My story is about a domestic terrorist who wants to blow up the shipyard or maybe the Seabrook nuclear power plant. I'm not really sure yet. I just know he wants to blow some shit up. You can find your way out." Charles nodded some more and made for the door.

Chapter 16

"So I've had to compartmentalize and really set some boundaries."

Charles heard a woman say this to her companion in Market Square several days earlier and could not get it out of his head. It was no use. Hearing the word "boundaries" had triggered the involuntary humor-composing mechanism that helped him take the edge off the looming specter of darkness that shrouded his entire existence.

He felt exhilarated because, now that he wasn't spending forty-plus hours a week burning brain cells on newspaper work, he had tripled his cognitive bandwidth for fresh creativity. Lately, there were moments when his idea flow felt positively manic, with aspects of a rocket ship ride; though he was wary of a possible *Dr. Strangelove*–style endgame. In such moments, he enjoyed the sensation that a particular item was writing itself in his head and that he was simply channeling it, sculpting it, in his capacity as co-writer and editor.

The piece coming at him now—one whose external force

pushed him from the kitchen to his writing desk—was a satiric exploration of the vocabulary we use and strategies we pursue to find fulfillment, or at least maintain our sanity, in a world gone haywire. He pictured it appearing under the "Shouts & Murmurs" heading in the *New Yorker*. "Boundaries" was his working title. Subtitle: "Meditations on living a jargon-filled life." He began typing:

Not long ago, I was a full-blown brain wreck—my "life" mired in a self-pitying vortex of botched diets, alcohol-fueled depression and medicinal blueberry pie a la mode.

Thank goodness, that on Thursday, Sept. 17, 2015, my once dear friend Jane recommended—or rather, insisted, for she was well-acquainted with my suffering—that I read an article on the subject of self-actualization.

Words on a page had never seemed so alive. They dared me to embrace their message that to reclaim my sense of identity and nurture the rebirth of my long-absent feelings of self-worth, I must conduct a thorough if painful emotional inventory, compartmentalize my rapidly metastasizing angst and fundamentally reorient my badly bruised consciousness to reject my worldview of whiny stoicism and embrace a lifestyle emphasizing personal responsibility and being truly present, i.e. living in the moment. That, in short, I must focus on me.

But just who is/was this alleged "me"? Is/was it/ he nothing more than a random, overweight mass of protoplasm loosely connected to something vaguely resembling a human spirit? Or was it/he more of a pathetic waste of a divine creator's effort to bestow the miracle of existence upon some undeserving loser?

This article (and I highly recommend *Unleashing Your Inner Ninja* to all, though I have long since transcended its, in retrospect, overly simplistic platitudes) opened my eyes to an entire universe of much more complex, cerebrally challenging and spiritually enriching… platitudes.

Though rising with the sun to practice the "Samurai I am" principles of ninja-hood (the wasabi breathing techniques, the surprisingly invigorating green tea enemas) fundamentally reshaped my reality, this would be just the first step on my journey of self-discovery.

The bracing process of reinvention moved me to deconstruct and reassemble my once-tattered psyche as something of a postmodern neonatal Aristotle, Dr. Seuss, Dale Carnegie hybrid. During this time, I intuited that my very survival also hinged upon being 99.4 percent gluten-free and immersing myself in cleansing rituals that included restorative autoasphyxiation, remedial mud dauber wasp therapy and, of course, peyote.

But as soon as I read *Sturm und Drang? Nein!*

by Gunther Hammerstein, I came to understand that my inner doppelgänger was utterly bereft of fahrvergnügen and that I must heed the incessant guttural voices narrating my ever-evolving bildungsroman so that I might gain a deeper understanding of how my innate weltanschauung related to the larger gestalt, and thus develop a healthier connection to the prevailing über-zeitgeist.

My now-insatiable appetite for brooding self-absorption led me to devour many of the popular and lesser-known "self-help" books in the public domain—*How to Alienate Friends and De-emphasize People*, *Harness the Rage Within*, *Frowning Tiger, Happy Dragon*.

These and others surely laid the metaphysical groundwork for my stream-of-consciousness phase. At once exhilarating and exhausting, it produced breakthrough-level revelations at a rate of approximately one every 17.5 seconds. During this period—characterized by synaptic frisson, breathless internal soliloquies and a heightened inability to distinguish between caregivers and caretakers—I gained significant insights into how I had allowed enablers and maddening codependencies to seize near-debilitating dominance over my previous, less-hypercognitive existence.

However, it was not until I read three more life-altering paperbacks—*101 Salvations*, *The Carbon Monoxide Orgasm*, and *Your Pillow Loves You*,

Know This—that I entertained even the slightest hint of skepticism toward these dime-store author-evangelists, with their me-centric mantras of mindfulness, karma-pooling and no high-fructose corn syrup after 8 p.m. Of course, I understand that less is the new more. But sometimes I wish they would stop insisting that I see the bottle of tequila as half full instead of half empty—when clearly, by any objective standard, it is completely empty. Again.

Finally, I learned to leverage my hard-won reservoirs of cognitive sapience to conceive my own system of self-perfectualization. At the risk of oversimplifying, it involves staring at the cosmic big picture with my third eye for 6-8 hours each day while emitting a didgeridoo-like drone from the diaphragm, deep down by the thorax.

By focusing an intense yet passive Taoist wu-wei mindset on negating all non-positivity, this transformative, sonically resonant anti-visualization technique ultimately empowers me to expand my once-earthbound consciousness to an omniscient state of universal strawberry pomegranate satyagraha.

There. Charles leaned back, laced his fingers together and pushed his palms out for a stretch. He briefly considered going back through, maybe try to think up some funnier book titles (*A Hitchhiker's Guide to Schizophrenia, Eight*

Habits of Highly Defective Douchebags), but it felt good to have pounded it out, non-stop, in under three hours so he resisted the urge to overthink it. *Fuck it*, he thought. *Print it out. Send it in.*

Chapter 17

Hope she's there, Charles thought as he walked to the post office carrying the New Yorker letter and a small package. While gathering the courage to approach Keri Ann's window, he examined a poster on the wall outlining the restrictions on what material can be sent through the mail. OK, this is it.

"Hi. I need to buy a stamp and mail this package."

"OK, how about Batman?"

Batman has been one of my heroes for as long as I can remember. He's dark and tormented like me, but way more cool and heroic. I could wow you with my encyclopedic knowledge of his epic battles with such archenemies as the Riddler, the Joker, the Penguin and Mr. Freeze dating back to his first appearance in Detective Comics No. 27, which sold for 10 cents when it was originally published in May 1939, but recently sold for $1.5 million. Did you know that when fired at full capacity, the engine of the 1995 Batmobile driven by Val Kilmer could shoot a 25-foot flame from the rear exhaust?

"Thank you. Batman will be fine." Charles thumbed the stamp onto the letter and slid the package across the counter.

"Wow, it's so light. What's in here?"

Actually nothing. Motivated by my desire to speak with you for longer than 6.2 seconds, I wrapped an empty box in brown paper and labeled it with an intriguing address. Hopefully, at this point I have engaged your curiosity about the fascinating stranger shipping a package to Arturo Slithergard c/o Dalai Lama Headquarters in Nepal. Though it contains nothing more than oxygen and two sheets of gift wrap tissue, it symbolizes what I hope you will one day come to regard as an adorable if slightly desperate scheme to meet you.

Charles wrestled himself from his internal monologue. "Oh, nothing. Definitely no explosives, flammables, or oxidizing materials, compressed gases, corrosives or radioactive materials. Certainly nothing that would violate Publication 52 of the United States Postal Service code."

Though the training manual carried explicit warnings about this kind of customer, Keri Ann's instincts told her he was harmless. "OK, that'll be $4.62."

Charles gave her a $10, but when she returned his change he stood motionless by the counter.

"Will there be anything else today?" she asked.

Would you like to run away with me? I'd charter a small plane or perhaps a helium balloon to carry us across land and sea to a champagne picnic on a tropical island, where our conversation would flow so effortlessly that it would soon become obvious that we were soulmates destined to spend eternity together, hand in hand, heart to heart.... And then we would kiss. And that, of course, would lead to something so wonderful that I dare not even imagine it, especially...

"Hello? Is there anything else I can help you with?"

Well, now that you mention it... Hey. Knock it off, dummy. Wrap this up before she figures out that you're a hapless lovestruck moron.

"No. Not today. Thank you so much for your hospitality."

Hospitality? Are you kidding me? Who says that? Try to force out the least insipid smile you can muster and get the hell out of here before you cause irreparable damage.

"No. Yes. Thank you."

"Alrighty. Have a nice day."

Now if he could just move his legs and walk away this would surely be one of the nicest days he'd experienced in at least two years.

"You seem like a deep thinker," she said. Pheromones gushed through his consciousness, his eyes widened and a smile danced, cheek to cheek, across his face as he tried to channel his elation into a graceful exit. "OK. Bye."

Keri Ann smiled to herself, cheered by the effect she was having on the shy, awkward gentleman. She had long since mastered the art of dodging subtle and overt come-ons from curious customers, but this felt like something entirely different. She tried to remember if she had seen him before. Yes, this Mr. Batman had a lost puppy dog, wounded soul aura that touched her inner nurturer. Plus, she chuckled, anyone who's corresponding with the Dalai Lama must be a peaceful spirit.

Chapter 18

"Damn, brother. Can't remember the last time I seen anybody get that excited about a smile. You must be pretty hard up. When was the last time you got some?"

Charles appreciated Stan's concern, but there was no way he'd be coughing up the truth, that it had been 12 years, 4 months and 17 days since he "got some." The encounter still haunted him, not that it wasn't pleasurable. It definitely "took the edge off" after his previous dry spell (6 years, 3 months and 29 days).

What were the chances that, while vacationing on the Maine coast, he would meet a hard-drinking nymphomaniac from Paris (the small mid-Maine town, not Hemingway's "movable feast" of culture, cuisine and creative inspiration) whose libido was powerful enough that she would not only tolerate, but fornicate with a sexually reticent anti-stud who could not stop talking about his existential crises du jour.

It's not that he didn't like sex. Um, loved it. However, he also found the entire process mortifying. First you have to actually *meet* a person you find attractive, for God's sake. His problem went way beyond fear of intimacy. No run-of-the-mill "bedroom jitters" for him. Shiver me timber. His condition was so severe that just thinking seriously about trying to have actual sex with an actual woman could bring on two straight weeks of genital night terrors.

"That long, eh? Man, we should take you out to the titty bar." Moments later, Charles was straddling the back of Stan's Harley racing south on Route One. Every aspect of this plan made him cringe inside, especially the idea of being in the same room with naked and semi-naked women. Sure, he was interested in their shapely silicon frontpieces, but his inborn sheepishness prevented him from relaxing and enjoying the show, and he nearly ran out the front door when a smoky-voiced brunette snuck up behind him and whispered, "You want a special dance, honey?"

He was trying to be a good sport, but within 15 minutes he was transfixed in mental exercises meant to stop himself from squirming. As a lover of word play, he found fleeting solace by focusing his attention on their names instead of on their bodies. Bambi, Brandy and Candy. Venus, Vixen and Desiree. They evoked flying creatures (Raven), fine automobiles (Porsche) and classy ports of call (here's looking at you, Malibu), even elements from the periodic table (really, Mercury?). Some of them were downright scary; a few were quite lovely. But looking, just for a second, at one of the youngest among them made him feel sad.

Just then, a crude loudmouth with a basketball-gut under his Bud Light shirt yelled something at the woman on the main stage. From his safe distance, Charles could not hear what the man said, but from the look on her face it must have been horrible because she stopped, knelt down to gather up the loose bills scattered at her feet, and clomped off the stage.

"You disgusting, misogynistic pot-bellied pig," Charles began. Stan sized up the situation and realized he'd made a mistake bringing his friend here. The poor guy was uncomfortable enough in his own skin without dragging him into a debaucherous, dimly lit lair of naked ladies and creepy losers.

He looked over at Charles and jerked his head toward the door. The two men gulped their last swallows of beer and hit the road. As they sped north, Charles felt his fingers start to twitch, a physical sign that a fresh blast of inspiration would require their presence at the keyboard. He closed his eyes and let the scene play out in his head— under the red, white, and blue Captain America helmet that Stan had provided for their X-rated road trip.

Once he was safely back in his home-like chamber of solitude, Charles whipped open his laptop and started rapping on the keys.

"What's your name, little man?"
  "Charles."
  "Hi Charles. What's your last name?"
  "Charles."

"OK, Charles Charles," said the policeman. "How come you look like someone just killed your dog?"

"Cause he did."

The boy had no proof that his father had killed his dog. But after seeing him beat Rascal as forcefully and frequently as he did, he was not buying the old man's story that the "goddamn mutt" had run off, never to return.

Charles had never confided with an authority figure, or any grownup, about the abuse he suffered at the hands of his father. But here was a possible window to rewrite history. To speak up instead of turning it all inward. Break the pattern of intricate, increasingly violent internal monologues and guarded restraint in what words were actually spoken—the pattern his subconscious created for him as a defense mechanism against getting beaten.

"Who killed your doggie, son?"

"My daddy. We live at 316 Turner Road. I'm Charles Manson." By now, the boy understood the impact he could deliver simply by saying his name out loud. The cop froze. Charles thought he even saw him take a half-step back.

Officer Simkins was proud that his job gave him the opportunity to make a difference in his community. Helping victims in car accidents, keeping drunks off the road—no problem. Investigate purse-snatchings, gravestone-tippings, missing child, cat up a tree. Whatever. But having some strange little boy tell you that he was Charles Bleeping Manson, son of a dog murderer—well, they didn't cover this kind of thing back at the academy.

"Can I give you a ride home, maybe talk to your dad."

"No thank you, sir."

Seriously, bring a cop home? That would be begging for a Category 5 ass-whipping. Instead, Charles thought, "Maybe you could just keep a close eye on that son of a bitch. Worst case, you'll know who to talk to if I turn up dead in the ditch that runs alongside our driveway."

Charles appreciated the policeman's kindness and felt bad about messing with his mind like that. Aw, who was he kidding? It was fun.

Chapter 19

"So what's your book about, Kerouac? Am I in it? I got some stories that'll make the short ones stand up on your nutsack. And I don't just mean crawling through the jungle straight out of high school. Biker wars. Vegas whores. Three to five for this or that. Needles. Bottles. Years lost under the influence. 1985? What's that?"

Stan wasn't in it yet, but Charles knew that if the novel came together the way he was hoping it would, a certain colorful Vietnam vet would definitely be a central character. Stan had come over to help him install his new kitchen sink. The old one had met an unfortunate accident—the faucet smashed and mangled, the stainless steel basin dinged and dented—when he finally funneled his anger about everything in the world into taking care of that relentless drip of water that had been Chinese water torturing him for several weeks. "Don't ask," said Charles, meaning the sink replacement job and not the book.

"Forget about it, psycho. We've all been there." As Stan muscled the new sink into place and began monkey-wrenching the pipes, Charles realized he actually wouldn't mind sharing a bit about the fictional version of his grim, cursed life story. He also knew that, in Stan, he could count on a brutally honest sounding board. "OK, I think it opens with me blowing up my childhood home and then reflecting on what an antichrist my dad was for the way he so thoughtfully, let's say, made me the man I am today. But then the reader sees I chickened out and didn't blow up a goddamn thing."

"Well, man named his boy Charles Manson Smith. Sounds like he deserves some fictional wrath-of-God payback. Get that shit out of your system, buddy," said Stan. "Hey, he still with us?"

"Oh, he's with us alright. In fact, he's right over there in the corner, cursing me. He's also up in my bedroom waiting for nightfall and he's down in the basement, hiding anything I go down there to look for and fucking with my fuses." Though his mind regularly facilitated fantasies about seeing his tormentor dead—the recurring rotting skull with the ridiculous comb-over being one of his favorites—Charles knew it was probably just wishful thinking. "No clue if he's dead or alive. Haven't seen him in decades," he said. "But I'm pretty sure that, in the novel, he's going down. Just not sure how yet."

Stan had seen enough to convince him that Charles was deeply troubled—and not some run-of-the-mill "aren't we all" bullshit. They didn't come up the with term post-traumatic stress disorder until long after Stan had hung up his uniform. But Charles' demons seemed dug in way deeper. It made him feel protective of his friend. "OK, try it now," he said. Charles nudged the lever on his new faucet to the right and cold water came gushing out. He smiled and nodded to Stan as he put his hand under the stream.

Charles hated it when his anger cost him money. Both mentally and economically, "losing it" and causing damage to his own property was bad for the bottom line. It also reinforced his general disgust in himself, and thus made him even angrier. He'd certainly spent more than a few moments deconstructing the idea that an individual act of anger could have consequences that caused even more anger—all part of a self-made, self-perpetuating cycle of self-destruction.

For example, if ketchup spurting across his hamburger, over his side pickle and onto his napkin and the kitchen counter caused anger that prompted him to whip his fork into the sink, breaking a glass; and if the broken glass caused a cut on his hand requiring stitches; and if driving to get stitches at the emergency room while enraged caused a car accident… well, it is easy to see how such a sequence could spiral out of control.

As a deeply introspective, high-functioning rage-aholic, he knew that anger was really nothing more than complex neurological forces creating an emotional response related to one's psychological interpretation of external and/or internal stimuli. But try telling that to those pissed-off little bastards inside his head who never let him have a moment's peace. He could try playing mind games with his limbic system, experiment with asserting conscious control over his amygdala until he was blue in the face, but it never stopped him from feeling like a pathologically ill-tempered being whose fury would one day be his undoing.

The idea of anger management counseling also made him irate. A quick review of the pricing structure common in this racket revealed that the typical anger management facilitator charged $250 per hour for one-on-one training. Instead, Charles employed various methods of self-therapy. Lately, he had been making an even greater effort to observe the inner turmoil that constantly besieged his strife-torn mind from an external perspective, much like an embedded reporter covering a war zone. Why, in the human experience, did anger manifest itself in symptoms that include teeth grinding, muscle tensions, prickly sensations, numbness, sweating and changes in body temperature?

Yes, the human mind is a fascinating and frightening organ, Charles thought, as he used two fingers of each hand to massage his temples. And lately his mind had begun to act a little funny—though, in truth, sticklers for accuracy might question his use of the word "lately." He was used to being buffeted by internal forces, hearing voices, even experiencing intense migraines. But this was different. What had once been a somewhat tolerable phenomenon that reminded him of a broken record, a sound or thought skipping and repeating inside his head, had more recently evolved into something more like the staccato skipping of a heavy metal CD.

Chapter 20

"Recognizing you have a problem is the first step, right?" As usual, his hateful, half-witted bathroom mirror failed to respond. Serving as both patient and therapist in his latest self-analysis session, Charles was once again urging himself to seek solace in activities that others consider soothing or relaxing. The idea of a Zen garden came to mind. However, also playing the role of devil's advocate, he countered that his personal experience seemed to confirm that any conscious quest for serenity inevitably brought on increased frustration and conflict. For example, taking a stroll in the park or sitting in the sun to sip a cup of coffee would often backfire tenfold.

Nevertheless, determined not to surrender to negativity, he decided to drive over to the garden center to purchase an executive desktop-style Zen garden and one of their finest bonsai trees. The exquisite little sandboxes with their dark wood exteriors really were quite lovely and he could understand why, in the pursuit of a meditative mindset, some people swore by them. His would be peopled by a small, rotund, bald Buddha figurine. It occurred to him that the tiny rake was far too small for him to accidentally step on one end and have it swing up and strike him in the face or crotch. He selected a wee juniper bonsai tree and headed for checkout. "Time to take you 'Om,'" he said to the contents of his shopping cart.

As soon as he merged onto the highway he knew he might have a problem. Another driver had been tailgating him ever since he exited the parking lot and he intended to break character for once and let the offense slide. But now this chrome-sniffing jackass was right on his back bumper. Charles felt a spark of road rage kicking in and he knew that if he did not find a way to extinguish it quickly, it surely would erupt into a full-blown wildfire. He pictured a sunny meadow next to a rippling brook, as a light breeze ruffled the tall grass and fluttered the leaves of the trees. He envisioned soft baby lambs—no; whiny voices, too annoying—kittens silently frolicking in the field as a rainbow traced a gentle arc into the brilliant blue sky.

The anger was not fully subdued, but it was ramping much more slowly than would typically be the case, so he continued the mental exercise. He paused and decided to try a new technique he had seen recommended by some armchair inner-stillness guru on TV. He could almost hear her voice whispering for him to take a long, deep breath, hold it for a moment, and then slowly exhale.

"Imagine you are standing on a white sandy beach. It's early in the morning, and a light, hazy mist surrounds you.

The sun is rising slowly. You can feel the warm, golden light on your face. You are feeling content. At ease. Relaxed… The sand beneath your bare feet is soft and warm. A gentle breeze caresses your face. Listen to the ocean as its waves break softly on the shore. As you walk slowly to the water's edge, you are feeling completely at peace and safe, as the currents create a gentle rocking motion that relaxes you even more deeply. The sun is now higher in the sky, its rays even warmer, and you watch as the mist that surrounds you begins to evaporate. Now you can see clearly in all directions. It is as though a veil has been lifted."

Gazing into his rearview mirror, Charles could see the pissed-off face of the driver in the vehicle that seemed to float just inches behind him. He could still feel the anger trying to sneak in and disrupt his reverie. So he decided to begin chanting his new mindfulness mantra, which was: "Fuck you, you hump-faced, cock-brained, dog-boning son of a motherless Clorox jug!"

The other driver pulled up next to him on the right and gave him the finger while shouting as he lowered his window. Charles returned the hand gesture and was working up a fresh barrage of invective when the man went silent and raised a pistol in his right hand, then pointed it. Charles stomped on the brakes as the other car sped past, then pulled over and waited for his heart to stop pounding. He flapped his head from side to side, like a dog drying itself after a dip in the lake, drew a deep breath and blew it out, adding a "woooo!" sound effect to help diffuse the adrenaline. He was shaken by the incident, his mind now flooded with stories and headlines he'd read about freeway free-for-alls escalating into gunfire.

"Florida man slays two in road-rage shootout."

Charles had always believed he could hold his own amid the jockeying, jousting, gesturing, screaming combat that characterized modern-day concrete jungle warfare. But he just realized this was a whole different ballgame and the rules had changed. No fair to be flipping birds and pointing fingers while adversaries were pointing pistols. Well, at least he still had the Zen garden. What could possibly go wrong in that tiny oasis of tranquility?

Before heading home, Charles tweaked his itinerary to squeeze in a quick little pit stop at the gun store. When he walked in, just for fun, he affected a cocky swagger, as if he was pushing through the swinging doors of an Old West saloon, seeking some desperado who done him wrong. But as soon as he walked in his demeanor changed and his feet stopped moving just inside the door. He had never seen so many guns, nor did he know a lot about them. In fact, he used to believe there was no place in his life for firearms, occasionally joking that, when it came to guns, he would just as soon A) never shoot one, and B) never be shot by one. But now the world was so screwed up he'd begun to think one might come in handy someday.

The display of firepower was overwhelming—walls and racks stacked with rifles, glass cases loaded with pistols. Some looked super cool while others just scared the shit out of him. He had read about the AR-15—apparently very popular for school shootings and other mass slayings—and he wanted to see one in person. Looking around the large, square room of death, he also wondered if they had Uzis, like the one that 9-year-old girl was firing when she lost control and killed the shooting range instructor in Arizona.

Like so many people, Charles had become numb to the gun violence that claimed the lives of children, and grownups, every single day in a country apparently too dumb to do a damn thing about it. Thinking his only weapon was the pen, he'd fired off a few shots in one of his newspaper columns—venting his frustration that, after Newtown, an overwhelming percentage of Americans favored expanded background checks for handgun purchases, but when it came to passing laws aimed at protecting people—shocker—Congress could only shoot blanks.

Charles quickly learned that making a public peep about such life-and-death matters meant painting a bull's-eye on your back. His "Questions About Firearms? Ask Professor Gunn" satirical advice column had inspired dozens of letters to the editor—some with subtextual hints of violence, others sounding straight-up sinister. One writer threatened, "I have more guns and ammunition than most 3rd world countries, and I'd love to give you a closer look, if you know what I mean." Others accused him of "smear, distortion, hate and lies," called him a "senseless (bleep) hole." Their bullet points included: "ignorant, appalling, vile and incendiary." Even "racist." Among the less literate, one labeled his work "drivvle," another wrote that he must be an "imbicle." Many called for him to be fired.

Now he was standing there in Guns R Us—still stunned by his country's refusal to lift a finger to minimize the carnage. But flexing his First Amendment rights had left him feeling impotent, even vulnerable. So maybe the Second Amendment could provide a remedy. He raised his right hand, extended his index finger and made eye contact with the man behind the counter.

"Can I help you?"

"Are you talking to me?" Charles half-whispered.

"What? I said, can I help you?"

Yes sir, I believe you can. I'm looking for something capable of mowing down every living creature within a 200-yard radius. And I want to look super badass doing it. I'm talkin' full metal Rambo. I want to lay waste to as much humanity as possible, get the death toll up nice and high. Maybe even go for the record, cause I'm feeling lucky. So gimme multiple magazines with maximum capacity, but minimal questions about my mental capacity. Punk.

As usual, he muzzled such thoughts. "Thanks, just looking… for now."

Chapter 21

Charles had been standing outside Lt. Quentin's front stoop for at least five minutes staring at the ornate wrought-iron spider hinges when the thick wooden door finally creaked open.

"You're 12 seconds late. Let's get to work."

Quentin gestured to a pistol-shaped remote control device in a holster strapped to his belt and bragged that the surveillance system inside his heavily fortified, centuries-old home was "state of the art."

"This little beauty controls the whole operation," he said, gesturing to the device. Part TV remote, part smartphone, probably part stun gun for all Charles knew.

"Surveillance, heat, lights. Music." He pushed a button and the voice of Frank Sinatra flooded the room in rich, textured surround sound.

Quentin cut the music and continued. "This screen gives me a live feed of every corner of the compound—every room, the grounds outside; I can watch you take a piss if you go to the bathroom. Cup of tea, I push this button here. Snifter of single malt, I use the voice option—Liquor. Cabinet."

A large canvas print of Manet's *A Bar at the Folies-Bergere* swung into the room, revealing three well-stocked shelves. Illuminated from behind, the bottles looked dazzling in the secret cabinet. Charles began scribbling notes. Good material for a scene in whatever over-the-top tale this nutbag wants to tell.

"Drink?" Quentin had two glasses and was pouring himself a Laphroaig. Charles wasn't much of a mid-morning drinker, but the entire tableau—the glistening hidden bar, the mahogany countertop, the mystique of the 18-year-old scotch—was too enticing to resist. He nodded.

"Mmm, love that smell," Quentin said as he lifted the glass to his nose then took a sip. "We're both mercenaries, Charles. I hired myself out to the military, then the police, with plenty of rogue ops along the way. Now you're hiring yourself out to me. I'm not sure where this story is going. But I do know I want to literally put the fear of God into people. They think those Al Qaeda a-holes were scary? Wait until they get a load of me."

Charles had no idea if Quentin knew he was quoting Jack Nicholson as The Joker in director Tim Burton's 1989 *Batman* starring Michael Keaton as the Caped Crusader. But the raw ego oozing from his statement was helping him get his head around the protagonist, while offering clues about the appropriate tone for the story to come.

"Terror, my friend. That's what we're talking about here. Real-time, bombs-blazing, shit-your-pants and turn-on-each-other terror. I want a rocket. Ripping toward a high-value target. I want epic explosions. Government in chaos. Revolution in the streets. Anarchy, baby! Give me anarchy, or give me death."

Jesus, now he's paraphrasing Patrick Henry while channeling Osama bin Laden.

"When I strike the nuke plant or the shipyard—blow up that stupid dome or a couple reactors on those Navy submarines—Uncle Sam won't know what hit him or what gets hit next. Then all hell breaks loose."

Charles was riveted, but also confused and increasingly concerned about his benefactor's mental well-being. "OK, when you say 'I,' I assume you mean the protagonist—this psycho, revolution fantasist, domestic terrorist."

"Duh! Don't interrupt. You getting the flavor of this?" Charles sat back, took a slug from his glass and continued taking notes.

"OK, now imagine the sound of a helicopter. It gets louder, louder, angrier. Something horrible's about to happen, you can feel it. It's like Hitchcock meets Coppola." Huh? Whoa. Charles didn't think it was possible for another human being to freak him out, but this shit was getting a little *Rear Window*-ish.

"What's the matter, Manson? Am I scaring you?" Quentin laughed. "Maybe you want to take a bathroom break." Charles shook his head and readjusted himself in his chair.

"Look, I love helicopters. Maybe you've heard about my new company out at the airfield—Attention Choppers. We charter tourist flights all over the region. I think I'd like to take you for a ride. It'll help you write my book, maybe visualize the movie version too."

"*Goddammit! So you're the son of a bitch that's rotor-tilling inside my head with those fucking red helicopters,*" was not what Charles said out loud, of course. He paused and studied the man who was finally taking a break from his manic narration and said, "By all means, let's you and I go for a ride."

Chapter 22

Stan was squinting, seemingly deep in thought as he hooked both thumbs into the belt line of his jeans and yanked, then adjusted his groin.

"You got a bucket list, Charlie? I know you're a little young for that shit, but some guys like to jump out of a plane, drive a fancy sports car, run with the bulls..."

Get through one 24-hour stretch without being utterly disgusted by nearly every aspect of my miserable existence? Charles' face tightened and he squirmed in his all-weather, plastic porch chair.

"You know what I mean. I know you're not the climb Mount Everest or bang a porn star type, but maybe you always wanted to swim with the dolphins, see the Statue of Liberty, go to fucking Disneytown or some shit."

Maybe banish my goddamn demons once and for all by going out in a blaze of glory? "I don't know, Stan. Publish a book I guess."

"Oh, I got faith in you, Charlie. Whatever you're cooking up, I see you going straight to the top of that New York

Post best-seller list. I used to think it would be cool to learn the violin. Achingly beautiful instrument, yeah? Reminds me of someone I once knew," Stan paused, as if letting a long-forgotten memory flicker through his mind. "Either that or the banjo."

Sitting on the $7 Walmart chairs and sipping beer in his dinky back yard, Charles looked up to the kitchen window and saw Elmer staring out. If there's one other thing that little guy might wish was different, he thought, he'd probably want to be an outdoor cat for just one day, maybe a long weekend. He imagined Elmer's bucket list: Catch a mouse, take a crap in the wilderness instead of always pooping into a plastic pan filled with tiny pebbles, maybe climb a tree and look down at his world from an aerial perspective.

The sound of a helicopter growled in the distance. Now getting louder, louder. Soon it was directly overhead. Its bulb-shaped cockpit was bright red. The two men squinted into the afternoon sky. Rather than waste brain cells on another inner jeremiad about noise pollution and man's never-ending war on simple peace and quiet, Charles instead focused on pretending he could use telekinesis to crash the chopper into the ocean. "You don't like those very much do you, Charlie? I can tell by the way you look at them."

"No, but I might be going up in one soon."

Stan put his right fist next to his heart. "Man, I'd kill to get up there one more time before…" His voice trailed off.

"Before what?"

"Nah. Before the old Grim Reaper comes knocking I

suppose." Stan started strumming some invisible strings while *dinga-ding ding ding ding ding ding ding ding-ing* the first few notes from "Dueling Banjos." He looked back up at the helicopter. "Hey, does it ever seem to you like those choppers spend a helluva lot of time buzzing those tourists over the shipyard?"

"Sure, I guess so. Hey, does anyone really call you Apocalypse?"

"No that was just a nickname a friend of mine gave me cause I'm a *craaazy* Vietnam vet," Stan swirled his finger next to his ear, "with the last name Nowell."

The two men had moved their powwow into the living room. Charles flipped on the TV and then immediately turned it off because the news was on, and it always got him upset.

"No, turn it back on. I want to see that," said Stan. The newsman was talking about the geopolitical hot spot du jour.

"As armed conflict and famine continue to consume Yemen," the anchor-hole said from the safety of his New York studio, "there is growing pressure for the Pentagon to commit to putting some boots on the ground."

Charles had become increasingly agitated by TV news readers using the term "boots on the ground" as a throwaway term to describe U.S. servicemen and women. Instead, he thought, let's call this what it really is. "On the ground" means in a war zone where one can die at any moment. "Boots" means people—people serving in the U.S. military. "God, I wish they'd stop calling brave men and women being shipped to a war zone 'boots'."

"I know what you mean, Charlie. But as a former 'boot,' it really is what you are. I mean, to the politicians sending you to wherever the latest shitstorm is, you're just a goddamn boot. You're sure as hell not a person, definitely not a human being. So I guess I got no problem with boot. I'll tell you what does bug me though, when those TV news-wads jabber about being 'on the ground' themselves—like, 'We're here, on the ground, reporting live from the fucking strawberry festival.'"

Charles shared his friend's revulsion at pompous television clowns trying to make their world sound more important by appropriating the language of war for their insipid soundbites. He imagined the strawberry festival reporter ducking mortar fire, strawberry syrup streaming down his face, crapping his pants as he scrambled for cover behind the fried dough tent.

Chapter 23

Dragging that little rake through the sand felt soothing. Charles spritzed his bonsai tree and raked straight rows from one end of the box to the other. Then he smoothed the sand and traced a yin-yang symbol. He rubbed the Buddha's bald head and belly. Yes, he found all of this very relaxing—until a fat house fly dropped by and invaded the scene.

First it lighted on the bonsai tree, probably delivering a payload of several hundred different kinds of bacteria. Having done his homework on these beastly parasites, Charles made a special effort to keep them out of his living quarters. The little bastards carry diseases on their legs, mouths and the small hairs that cover their disgusting bodies, transferring microscopic particles of God knows what after dancing and buzzing around feces, garbage and rotting animal carcasses.

According to his research, diseases carried by house flies include typhoid, cholera and dysentery, salmonella, anthrax and tuberculosis. Highly effective at depositing these pathogens on food or touched surfaces, they are also skilled at transmitting the eggs of parasitic worms, probably herpes and syphilis, too, for all he knew.

Charles was certain that the housefly was staring at him, taunting him, with its beady, compound eyes. He knew its thousands of individual optic lenses and quick reflexes made it extremely difficult to swat. Now it was getting cocky. Perched on top of the Buddha's head, it began grooming itself, using its forelegs to primp itself for the impending showdown.

"You're trespassing, mister. I'm going to have to ask you to leave." The fly did not budge. Charles thought it might have even wiped its ass before setting all six legs back on the statue, poised for emergency takeoff. He first tried to use his meditative, faux kung fu prowess to swoop in and snatch the fly in midair as it made its escape. Charles swiped his hand toward the fly—and swatted the Buddha statue straight through a pane of glass in his living room window. Still thinking he might have caught the fly, he shook his hand, then made a throwing motion toward the table, hoping to stun or kill his prey. Empty.

There it was. Over by the window. Now bumping into the wall before doing a dipsy-doodle over by the T.V. Quiet. When Charles looked back at his garden and saw the fly standing on his rake, he was overcome with an urge to smash it to hell. Then run for the anti-bacterial hand soap. *Bam!* The sandbox flew off the table, as the fly navigated through the thousands of tiny particles that came to rest on Charles' table, couch and carpet.

The uprooted bonsai tree was now peeking out from under the sofa. Charles screamed at the fly, which he had tracked to the inside of a lampshade. He grabbed a dark green yard waste bag from the closet, swung it over the lamp and began bludgeoning his table, destroying the lamp and filling the bag with light bulb shards. When Charles emptied the bag onto the table, the fly was there amid the rubble. It had sustained injuries to its head, wings and abdomen. He entertained the idea that it might also have suffered a massive coronary.

But just as he was about to squash it with a napkin and dispose of it once and for all, it jolted back to consciousness and flew out the hole in the window it had just helped create. Charles hunched himself into a half-crouch, gripped a fistful of denim and quadriceps in each hand and unleashed one more cathartic scream before going to the medicine cabinet, shaking out two ibuprofen and inhaling them with a saliva chaser.

Chapter 24

Charles pulled out a shopping cart and double-checked his list as he walked toward the entrance to the grocery store.

> Ground beef.
> Avocado.
> Almonds.
> Fresca.
> Eggs.
> Extra sharp cheddar.
> Bag of spinach.
> Bacon.
> Bacon.
> Bacon.

In the weird halftime lo-carb world that he inhabited, Charles was a major consumer of bacon. No rationing of rashers for him. He'd even bought that crazy Bacon Bowl they used to show on TV—filled 'em up with scrambled eggs, salads, burgers.

When he passed the sensor that triggered the automatic door, it began to open—but, as happened every time, it moved far too slowly to accommodate his brisk, lengthy strides. So he gave it a little shove and a piece of his mind. *Move it, glassy. Fucking pane in the ass.*

As he began gathering supplies in his cart, he spotted Keri Ann in the pet food aisle. And froze. In the 3-5 seconds before he could regain control of his limbs and torso, five thoughts flashed through his panicked mind:

1. Slowly step away from the cart, and get out of here; no. 2. Go directly to checkout and try to skulk away without her noticing; no. 3. Would she even remember the oddball who bought the Batman stamp and shipped the mysterious, freakishly light package to Nepal? Iffy. 4. Resume shopping and act casual if the natural flow of events caused them to cross paths. Yeah right. 5. Stalk her and choreograph a "chance encounter," most likely in the frozen foods aisle, where if he could sidestep disaster during a polite exchange of mundane pleasantries, he might dare to deliver a hastily written script suggesting that they get together somewhere, someday.

Uncharacteristically bold, yes. But this was Keri Ann. He had no idea what his feelings were, but he knew he had some. Oh, God. "Hey, it's you, P.O. Box 562. How did that Batman stamp work out for you?"

Her smile floored him. Not literally, of course. But it went right through him, making him feel warm, even a bit flushed. Definitely not cool. Anxious and at least a little bit terrified. "Good." *C'mon moron. Say something more than, good. This is your big chance, lover boy. Don't blow it. She was still smiling.* "How... are you today?"

"Oh, not too bad. When you work at the post office, any day away tends to be pretty OK."

Sweet poetry. "I'm shopping," said Charles.

"What a coincidence, me too." She had a sense of humor, a graceful touch that she must find particularly helpful in easing otherwise awkward exchanges with dopey, socially inept admirers.

"I have to get going," he said. *Say it. C'mon dummy, spit it out. This might be your only chance.* He paused, blinked slowly, then actually looked into her eyes. "Would you like to go for a bike ride sometime?" He was fairly shocked that he had managed to blurt out the words, but straight-on flabbergasted by her enthusiastic response. "Sure, how about Sunday? Meet you at noon in the square?"

"Yes!" Charles feared he might have yelled out the word with a dangerously high-pitched infusion of glee. "See you then." He turned and made a beeline for the express lane.

After speeding home, Charles went down to the basement to check on the condition of his bicycle. He enjoyed riding—a long time ago. It was still black, with white lettering, fifteen speeds, eight or nine of 'em still working last time he checked. A mountain bike with wide knobby tires, it was pretty much state of the art when he bought it for $339 about thirty-five years ago. Dust, cobwebs, a small spider making its home amid the spokes on the rear wheel.

He rolled it out. The tires were dead flat, as expected,

so he used the hand pump to reinflate them to forty-nine, fifty, fifty-one, fifty-two pounds of pressure. He gripped the handlebars, swung his leg over the saddle and sat down. Tires seemed solid. He would need a serious test ride—and way more elaborate mental preparation—before Sunday's meeting with Keri Ann. At least one part of this would be easy. Portsmouth provided spectacular scenery for a bicycle excursion. He wheeled the bike out the door and onto the sidewalk—then paused.

He did not mean to imagine himself on a tiny bike, training wheels freshly removed, his father with his hand on his shoulder. But it was too late. His grip felt unsteady as his father began pushing him, while filling his left ear with an Miller High Life-scented pep talk. "C'mon, don't blow this, you lazy little bookworm. Do this right, or I swear to God…"

He gave an aggressive shove and Charles immediately felt as if he had zero control over his wobbly steed. He veered left, then right, before careening hard into the neighbor's garbage cans, knocking loose the lids and soiling himself with miscellaneous kitchen waste and coffee grounds. The old man's laugh lasted only about half a minute, morphing straight into an X-rated berating. Charles felt grateful to escape a beating, as his mother came outside to triage the scene and clean him up. Ah, memories.

Charles had been looking forward to rolling along the waterfront, out toward the old fort by the Coast Guard station, and on to the little town park with the immense, sloping lawn and the tiny town beach. He used to love to stand on the lonely stone jetty and gaze out at the lighthouse, the island holding up an empty, run-down home from another century, the giant tankers he imagined brimming with mysterious cargo from faraway lands.

He pushed off from the curb and was overcome with how freeing it felt to roll, under his own power, away from his world of troubles toward a more peaceful place set amid scenery so idyllic and timeless that it was easy to imagine it as an N.C. Wyeth or Winslow Homer painting. As he cycled through the South End toward the small bridges and the open stretch of road lapped by water on both sides, he felt a strong breeze that made him tighten his grip and pedal a bit harder. Within moments, wind was whipping his chest and face, slowing his pace almost to a crawl. Charles hated to have a ride ruined by these kinds of conditions and soon, with no one near to hear him, he was howling out loud at the wind. "You suck! Why can't you let me ride in peace! Blooowww meeee!"

The wind buffeted him for another five minutes until he reached the relative shelter on the other side of the open-water stretch of his journey. He ejected himself from the bike and pushed off, running as it rolled then tumbled into a ditch. He kicked it, striking the back tire and hurting his foot, causing a fresh outburst of anger. With most of his rage now expelled, Charles put his hands on his knees and panted, glaring at the bike until he cooled down enough to grab it roughly and continue on his way.

Now pedaling smoothly once more, he cursed himself for letting the wind cause his latest seizure of temporary insanity. It's air, for fuck's sake, the very oxygen your body needs in order to exist. No reason to bust a lung yowling at it. Sure pal, tell it to the goblins screaming inside your head.

Chapter 25

Still agitated about the goddamn wind, Charles said a silent prayer for calmer conditions on Sunday then sat down next to the laptop to work on his novel. Some of his memories were so visceral that he often felt it was easy to flip a switch and transport himself back in time...

"Your boy is extraordinarily bright, Mrs. Manson. His test scores place him in the 99th percentile," the principal told his mom.

"And yet he doesn't have enough sense not to climb out a second-floor classroom window, shimmy down some exterior piping and go monkey around on the jungle gym when he got bored during a lesson on Christopher Columbus," Charles, then nine, thought to himself while sitting next to his mother as the principal laid out her concerns about his behavior in school.

"But this latest incident has us very concerned. He could have been seriously hurt. Taking into account that after the thing with the crayon, his fixation on the aquarium, that drawing he made..."

Ah yes, the drawing. Certainly, his grasp of proportion and perspective could use a little work. But the house, he felt, was a fairly accurate representation of the brick, ivy-covered home he shared with his parents and brother. And he actually felt somewhat proud of his use of shadow to imply a sense of something sinister.

OK, his mom—despite her round eyes and flat crescent moon smile—looked haggard, forlorn and unnecessarily angular, a splotch of red just below the capital M on her apron. And his brother—a mini Mr. Potato Head assemblage whose crude linear appendages and white-mittened hands seemed almost an afterthought—was definitely amateur hour.

But he felt the focal point of the piece, the great beast that towered over the house—part raging minotaur, part fire-breathing gargoyle—was rather epic for such an artistic neophyte.

It had sprung from palette to paper in a crayon-ic cyclone of mad inspiration—a mutant, bellowing ogre with bolts protruding from its neck next to its thick, python-like jugular vein—etched against a scorched-earth backdrop tinged with soylent greens and clockwork oranges.

The tone of the piece sought to suggest ominous contrast between the white-picket façade and the tense psychological hellscape that was his father's contribution to domestic life at 316 Turner Road.

How did the teacher and principal not recognize A) his innate talent, and B) his agonizing internal struggle manifesting itself in C) this textbook case of a troubled child's cry for help?

"Mrs. Manson, we all like Charles. But he is often sullen and disagreeable. This makes the other children uncomfortable and sometimes they channel those feelings by teasing him—often about his name."

Yes, the cruelty dished out by influential figures in his peer group undeniably impacted his socialization and sense of self-regard. "Little Charles Manson, he's the devil's grandson." That gem courtesy of Jimmy Finnegan, playground bully, statistically just as likely as Charles to snap one day and wind up behind bars.

"Of course, we want to do everything we can to work with you to help Charles succeed." Clare Manson averted her eyes as the principal transitioned to the obvious. "Is everything OK at home?"

"Yes, of course. He is a handful, but we're doing the best we can. You are so kind. Thank you for your efforts to help Charles fit in."

In the car, his mom was quiet, waiting until the station wagon had pulled out of the school parking lot before she finally spoke.

"Don't worry. We won't tell your father about this. Let's just go home and make you a peanut butter and jelly."

Chapter 26

Charles had come to hate the sound of skateboards vibrating across his street and sidewalk. Punks.

He looked outside just in time to see them disappearing from his view. As Elmer joined him at the windowsill, something moved Charles to walk out front for a quick look-see. From the front stoop he spied what looked like several flyers fluttering from a telephone pole. Next to an eight-by-eleven-inch sheet appealing for help finding a missing beagle, he saw his own face.

"FBI's Most Wanted List—Charles Manson Smith"

For one of two mug shots they reproduced the picture that used to run with his column in the paper. But where the hell did they get that side-view shot?

"Wanted for first-degree craziness and suspicion of being a douche."

Charles could not help but chuckle.

"Warning: Do not attempt to subdue this penis-head."

Then, in bigger type: "If you see this man sniffing your garbage can or yelling at your dog, please run back into your house and contact your local FBI office."

He had to give them a few points for creativity. They must have gone online and mimicked some of the phrasing from a wanted poster—even googled an official-looking FBI logo and Photoshopped it onto the document. But they had already pulled this gag with the "Beware: Homo gay sex offender psycho" flyer. Thirteen years old and already losing his edge. About twenty-four hours later, though, he revised his assessment when Agents Phillips and Winchester knocked on his door. As in their previous visit, Agent Phillips did the talking.

"Mr. Charles Manson Smith. Again."

"Agents."

"I thought we were very clear about not wanting to ever come back here to see you again. But then the boss gets a call from an old man responding to a wanted poster, saying he knew the exact whereabouts of Charles Manson Smith.

"A little puzzling at first. But when we interviewed your neighbor and he showed us the poster, we managed to put two and two together and figure out it was a fake. What we don't understand is: Why are there a dozen-plus wanted posters with your name and face on them popping up within a half-mile radius of your house?"

Oh, that's because I'm a stone-cold, natural-born psycho whose long-simmering madness has now escalated to the point where I'm on the brink of losing it and going on a three-state satire spree. But that's just my theory. To get the real story, you might need to waterboard a couple of juvenile delinquents.

"Don't know," said Charles. "Neighborhood pranksters?"

"I really don't like you, pal," said Phillips. "And if we ever have to come back here again, you're not going to like us very much either. Got it?"

Not to worry. Phillips, is it? Your arrogant, condescending attitude and general air of contempt have already filled me with enmity. So go fuck yourself, and then go fuck the corpse of J. Edgar Hoover.

Charles touched his right ear, as if picking up a signal from an invisible transmitter and then said, "OK, goodbye." About 15 minutes later, Stan rolled up on his Harley and Charles invited him inside for a cold Pabst.

"Jesus, Charlie, the feds stopped by again? Glad I wasn't there," said Stan. Charles agreed that—for at least a dozen different reasons, most of which he could only imagine— it was a good thing Stan hadn't been sitting in his living room when the agents stopped by.

"Once these guys have got you in their sights, it almost always means trouble," Stan warned. "Hate to tell you, buddy, but you're on their list now."

Chapter 27

Inside the helicopter, Charles was surprised to find himself unbothered by the cacophony that infuriated him when he heard it on the ground. Headphones muffled the noise as they prepared for takeoff with Quentin at the controls. Once aloft, what was left of the noise was rather soothing, if only in the sense that as long as the engines were humming it reduced the odds of plummeting toward the earth and perishing in a fiery explosion.

Charles loved the perspective afforded by the altitude. Seeing his world from above, smaller than life, gave him a sense of being detached from it all instead of being stuck in the middle of all the mayhem. Of course, Quentin kept rupturing his reverie by barking at him to look at each of the region's countless landmarks—lighthouses, church steeples, skinny strips of shore-front sand.

"Here's Hampton Beach. We're almost to Seabrook." Quentin spent extra time looping the nuclear plant dome, in the name of research, he said, urging his ghostwriter to study its features and take notes that might be needed for the novel. Charles thought of the mission as a "fission expedition."

"Wonder what it would take to blow up that dome," said Quentin. "No way my helicopters could do it. Maybe an armed drone." Charles knew Quentin would want his villain to deliver some clever lines. So he decided to wordplay along. "Dome wasn't built in a day, but it'll be gone in sixty seconds."

"Hey, that's not bad," Quentin said. "You know, when this thing starts leaking radiation, sirens go off and the whole region gets evacuated. You might want to read up on caesium-137 and strontium-90, dirty bombs and potassium iodide."

When they finally started heading back up the short New Hampshire coastline, Quentin seemed eager to get to the shipyard. The base (est. 1800) launched its first warship in 1815 and had survived wars, nautical tragedies and multiple congressional attempts to shut it down.

A memorial flying the American flag atop a 129-foot pole commemorates the loss at sea on April 10, 1963, of the USS *Thresher* and all 129 of the men on board. Charles watched as the facility's warehouses, work bays and cranes came into view. But its most distinctive feature was a colossal castle-like structure that once served as a naval prison. "Look at this place. It's like a goddamn fortress," said Quentin.

Chapter 28

When his alarm went off, Charles sat bolt upright—5:55 a.m.—excited but nervous as hell. The bike was ready. The picnic supplies were ready. But he had serious doubts about himself. He felt he needed to muster at least a modest level of self-confidence, but he also knew that as soon as he got out of the shower, that asshole in the mirror was going to screw with him again. Elmer was sitting in his Sphinx pose on the bath mat, waiting for Charles to emerge. He was patient, having learned that his towering companion was in the habit of performing certain daily rituals before plopping a spoonful of shreds into his bowl.

When Charles pulled back the curtain and started the shower, Elmer stretched, did a quick circle, then moved into the hallway to claw his favorite carpet. Feeling the hot water on his head and back of his neck was always one of the highlights of his day. Rubbing shampoo into his scalp with vigorous intensity, he tried to put the already creeping negativity on hold so his mind could do a subconscious scan for dream snippets.

The bulk of his dream footage fell into two basic categories—1) searching for his missing car as frustration built to extreme anger and 2) getting locked in slow-motion as he tried to move with purpose toward any destination or goal. But this one was different. He was at some sort of writers conference in an old mansion or stately inn. Walking down the long hallway on the second floor, he looked into each room and saw seminars, lectures and dialogues on the beauty and complexity of human communication. As he considered ducking into one of the rooms to grab a seat in the back, he came to another doorway and looked inside to see a two-story room with a balcony overlooking an indoor pool. People were splashing and he felt compelled to join them.

Now clad in his brown swim trunks, he leapt over the railing and plunged into the warm, clear water. Under the surface, his slow motions felt soothing instead of frustrating. When he came up for air, he discovered the pool had given way to open water, perhaps a river, filled with people swimming back and forth in one wide lane. Now swimming too, sidestroke, he was building such speed in the choppy water that he kept almost bumping into people, noticing their surprised expressions as he darted out of the way to avoid a soft collision. The dream stopped there. Way too soon.

Charles grabbed his towel and rubbed his head back to reality. A dab of Colgate on his toothbrush, he felt repulsed that his teeth were borderline yellow. Those stupid whitening rinses were beyond useless, but at least they gave him a daily opportunity to spit a mouthful of metaphorical bile into the sink and down the drain. He also hated his hair—short and mostly brown, but grayer by the day. What he hated was that, even though he succumbed to the pressures of vanity and tried to gel or spray it, he could not prevent hundreds of individual strands from hanging down and fanning out over his forehead, creating an effect that made him feel more like some long-lost Dr. Seuss character than a man.

He nicked himself when he was almost done shaving and the sight of his own blood stopped him cold. To stanch the flow of macabre, self-destructive images, he tossed the razor back into the corner, splashed the spot of blood from his jaw and got the hell out of there.

Elmer, perched and waiting on the kitchen counter, stood and paced off a tight circle as Charles approached the refrigerator. Normally, he'd get some coffee going first, but the little guy had been patient as Charles lingered longer than usual over his morning, mirror-focused psychoses. He grabbed the can with the little spoon and moved toward the bowl.

"Meow," he said, while dropping in a dollop.

"Meow," replied Elmer.

Once the coffee was ready, Charles reached for a mug from the top shelf of his cupboard. When he saw that it bore the name and logo of his former newspaper, he flashed hot and smashed it on the kitchen floor.

His home bore the scars of similar activities. One of his shutters still had two slats cracked from the impact of a fast-moving frisbie. His bedroom door never closed properly after a particularly forceful slamming. A kitchen wall carried the long-ago stain of an apple flung with such fury that he strained his shoulder. The inside of his fridge went dark for five months after he slammed the door so hard that it extinguished the bulb and damaged the socket. And so on.

Charles planned to lead Keri Ann along his favorite waterfront path, stop at the old fort at the Coast Guard station and bust out a light picnic lunch, there or at the grassy town common. He had strawberries. Hummus, harvest wheat crackers and Jarlsberg cheese. Cranberry-pomegranate juices. And, a couple of fresh, fat North Atlantic shrimp with tangy horse radish cocktail sauce for dipping. All neatly packed with a thin blanket in his backpack.

He took a quick inventory and diagnosed himself with cold sweats, lukewarm shivers and jitters, trepidation, goose bumps and butterflies, pins and needles, mild to moderate heebies and acute jeebies.

"Stan. I'm supposed to meet Keri Ann for a bike ride at noon and I'm, uh, you know."

"Freaking out?"

"Yes."

Charles had called his friend for an anti-pep talk. Too much pep would only fuel his anxiety.

"Alright, buddy. Shhhhh. Take a few deep breaths. Slow it down. If you have a beer, crack it, take a few big swigs and pour the rest in the sink." Charles followed his friend's advice. "All you need to do is just relax, kick back and be yourself. Wait, strike that. Try to be that calmer version of yourself—that state of mind you're sometimes able to find when you're at home just chilling with Elmer.

"One thing you should know about nearly every woman, no matter how young or old, is that deep in her soul beats the sweet, hopeful heart of a sixteen-year-old girl. You've told me about Keri Ann. There's no threat here. Nothing to fear. You find a way to lose yourself in those pretty green eyes and your dumb-ass demons won't have a prayer."

Charles was near tears as he hung on his dear friend's every word.

Chapter 29

Keri Ann was already there when Charles rolled up to the square. God, she was beautiful. Blonde hair in a pony tail, cute sunglasses, stretchy yoga pants and a pastel fleece top. She had a nice mountain bike, too.

He was glad to see she brought a helmet because the road was narrow with cinders and steep shoulder, and the drivers whizzed by eyeing the boats and tall fishing birds. He never did, of course; smacking his head on the pavement might do him good, shake loose some of the toxins. Charles admired her as he walked his bike to the spot where she stood sipping a coffee. She glanced over, gave a big smile and waved.

"I hope you don't mind," she said, holding up her cup. "I came a few minutes early because I hadn't had any coffee today."

Aaaahhhh, maybe I shouldn't have downed that fourth cup this morning, he thought. *Take a deep breath and try to act normal when you speak.*

"Of course. I'm little bit hooked on my morning caffeine,

too." He even made a small joke by extending a trembling right hand. She smiled, not realizing that his right hand was actually trembling and had been for almost five minutes.

"Where shall we go?" Now his meticulous planning paid off, as Charles was able to relax into the moment and reel off a rough outline of their route, culminating with surprise "refreshments" at an undisclosed "scenic vista." They wheeled their bikes down toward the river and into the park. Charles thought about stopping to tell her about the statue of Ensign Charles Emerson Hovey but decided to save that for, he hoped, another day.

Swift currents flowed past the shipyard on the opposite shore, pushing upriver and under the bridge. The park offered three piers that poked out into the water, the biggest one with elevated wooden benches for river-watching. From here, they had a panoramic view of what Charles considered to be the very essence of New England life.

Gazing inland, the park itself was a treasure—its grounds teeming with green grass, a kaleidoscope of colorful plantings and a stage for outdoor summertime shows. Just beyond the park, antique buildings formed a historic village that invited visitors to imagine how lives were lived in a simpler time. To the left, salt-shaded vessels lashed to the commercial fishing pier offered a window into a working waterfront heritage that was still very much alive.

Continuing in a gradual counter-clockwise circle, an observer's personal periscope would spy the shipyard, symbolizing two-plus centuries of hard and important work, patriotism and pride. Looking slightly further left, the picture-postcard pirouette focused on the three bridges spanning the river, linking New Hampshire and Maine to each other and to the world beyond.

The river itself was a sensory delight—an environmental and economic ecosystem, ever bobbing with lobster boats, tankers and tugs. They were silent together for several moments as Charles tried to find the words to express his deep affection for this place. "It's beautiful, isn't it?" Keri Ann said. And he knew she understood.

They pedaled on, through the South End, past the fish market and the causeway, Quentin's house located just around the bend. A house covering most of a small island visible to their left. The first bridge was empty; folks fished off the second one. Gulls chattered. The breeze was light today.

The Coast Guard station stood on a peninsula behind a tall fence with a narrow gate. They squeaked their handlebars through and obeyed a sign ordering them to stay on a yellow line that led to the remains of a Revolutionary War-era fort, its inland face walled with brick. To their right, past cracked pavement marked as a helicopter landing spot, the mouth of the harbor opened to the sea.

Their tires bounced on cobblestone as they passed through an arch and rode across a grassy plain toward mammoth stones erected on the plateau at the river's edge. Charles had always been fascinated that the stonework featured window-like openings, embrasures, through which military weaponry was once fired at enemy ships.

Leaning out through one of the holes, their shoulders brushed as they looked straight down at the water lapping the rocks.

"Are you hungry?"

"Yes," she said. "What an ideal spot for a picnic."

Charles spread out the blanket at the edge of the grass and began unpacking their treats. "Ooh, strawberries," she said, smiling as he placed the rest of the feast between them. "I hope you like cranberry-pomegranate juice." After they twisted open their drinks, she proposed a toast.

"To new friendships."

"Yes, to new friendships."

As they touched the soft plastic containers together, a seagull dove into their airspace and snatched the small sandwich bag containing the cocktail shrimp. "What the…!?" Charles pushed back hard to try to block the flames from bursting out through his ears. "*You shrieking web-footed sea rat!*"

Even though he knew the shrimp were long gone, he briefly imagined himself leaping into the sky, grabbing the now-terrified scavenger by the neck in midair and punching it in the head. Keri Ann sensed his distress and yelled after the gull, "Hey, you forgot the cocktail sauce." Then she smiled at Charles and said, "That'll probably be the best meal he ever had."

Wow. He paused to analyze how quickly her easy sunshine had calmed him. As his heart rate dropped out of the danger zone, he winced out a quarter-smile and said, "Secure the strawberries and batten down the hummus."

Keri Ann laughed and even leaned against him in her mirth. Over the next half-hour he learned she was new to the area, here from Minnesota, still heart-deep in recovering from her split with a former nice guy who turned out to be a jerk. "Why do so many men... Never mind," she said. "You seem nice. Very different, but nice."

She reached over to touch his hand and when their eyes met, he prayed she would never find out just how "different." Being near her disarmed him, but also made him feel extra paranoid that he would do something to screw things up. At least he would always have this breezy afternoon; he imagined how he might memorialize the moment in his novel.

Chapter 30

Charles slept in the next morning, but greeted the day angry—awakened by a loud banging, then shouting. "Charlie, you home?" Stan was knocking hard on his door. "Charlie!" Charles opened the door and let him in. "Hey, can you give me a ride to Portland?" Even though he hadn't known him for very long, Charles figured he would have done just about anything for Stan.

"Sure, what's in Portland?"

"I need you to take me to my brother's house."

Something was off. Stan seemed agitated. Plus, it was only 6:30 and he knew Stan to be somewhat of a night owl.

"So, what's this all about?"

"Aaaah, I'll tell you on the way."

They went outside and walked toward Charles' ten-year-old black Honda Civic with the busted driver-side mirror. Stan eyed the mirror and Charles just shrugged and spit on the ground as they climbed inside. The backseat was littered with books, newspapers, jackets, loose clothing and broken sunglasses.

"Long story," Charles said as Stan's stare seemed to be seeking explanation for the missing mirror. He sure as hell wasn't going to regale Stan with the ugly details, but now he was fixated on the flashback.

He'd been driving along, minding his own business, when he felt an accumulation of phlegm in the back of his mouth. He tensed his esophageal muscles and made that sound people emit when preparing to spit, but the process went horribly awry. Some of the saliva-phlegm mix splattered his window, car door and mirror. And some of it bungeed back inside, smacking his left cheek and trailing down onto his shirt. So he lurched to the curb, leapt from the vehicle and karate kicked the mirror to the pavement, then stood over it glaring. Stan, who had been watching his friend silently revisit the trauma, just shifted his eyes back to the road ahead.

They had only driven a couple blocks when, no more than a hundred yards ahead, a police car sped into their path from a side road, lights flashing. Stan scrambled into the backseat and onto the floor where he tried to cover himself in the mess Charles kept back there. A cop emerged and signaled for Charles to roll down his window. "License and registration please."

Charles handed them over. The cop leaned in to look through a window and into the back seat of the dark, two-door coupe. Then he turned away and said something into his radio.

"What's this about, officer?"

"Why don't you let me ask the questions here?"

Here we go, thought Charles. From zero to a-hole in 5.2 seconds. He gripped the steering wheel with both hands, pursed his lips and exhaled slowly through his nose. "Hmmm, Charles M. Smith. Mr. Smith, we're looking for a man named Stanley Nowell." The officer held up a mug shot of Stan. "Have you seen this man?"

"No sir. Looks like a real psycho. What's he done?"

"Again, Mr. Smith, this will work best if you just let me ask the questions, OK? We got a report that he was spotted this morning in your neighborhood. Are you sure there isn't anything you'd like to tell us?"

"Not a chance, copper. You couldn't beat it out of me if you tried, cause Charles Manson Smith ain't no rat, see." Hey knock it off, Charles told himself, *this isn't funny.* "No sir."

The officer craned his neck to look in the backseat again. "OK, Mr. Smith. But if you see your friend, we're going to need you to call us right away." Wait a minute. My friend? Uh-oh. Charles's mind was reeling as he pulled away from the curb, watching the police in the rearview. "Stan? What the hell is this?"

"I'm a psycho, huh? Thanks a lot, Charlie." Stan poked his head up from under the pile of clothes. "Seriously though, thanks for having my back."

"Stan?"

"OK, yes. Five-oh is after me Charlie. Turns out, in their world, I'm a notorious narcotics kingpin. Real story, I sell a couple bags of weed to help make ends meet," he said, clambering back into the front passenger seat. "Come to think of it, you ever try any? Medicinally speaking, it's real good for everyday stress. Let alone whatever the hell freaky shit you're always dealing with."

Of course, he had tried pot. But he was really kind of indifferent about it. Some people say it mellows you out, but, medicinally speaking, it sure as hell never mellowed the unwanted high from the chemical neurotransmitters that made him feel, he imagined, more like a meth head on angel dust.

"Jesus, Stan. That was close. What…" His question was cut short by two more police cars, one nearly smashing into him from a side road on the left as Charles jacked on the breaks and screeched to a halt. A group of kids shooting baskets on a hard-topped court stopped what they were doing to watch the action.

"OK, Charlie," said Stan. "Just stay calm and everything's going to be fine."

The buzz of adrenaline lit up Charles' mind. Just stay calm—that's what the cops are supposed to say. Stan nudged open the passenger door and held his right hand high in the air. Slow and steady, he put one boot on the pavement, then the other, as he stood and stretched his left hand to the sky. "OK boys, you got me. I surrender."

Four officers swarmed him. Two slammed him into the Honda's hood and a third kicked his feet out from under him as they threw him face-down onto the street. Stan did not seem to be struggling. "You want some ID?"

When Stan, now handcuffed, reached for his back pocket to grab the wallet that was chained to his belt, the takedown turned even more chaotic. From the other side of the car, Charles witnessed what looked like a tangled blur of kicking, night-sticking and pistol-whipping as Stan convulsed from at least one blast from the taser.

"Don't move!" Frozen stiff, Charles had no intention of moving. But that didn't stop his mind from charging into the melee, overpowering three officers with secret ninja moves he never knew he possessed, subduing the fourth cop with his own taser, then disarming them all and lining their weapons up, out of reach, on the sidewalk. As they dragged Stan, now limp, into one of the cruisers, Charles pictured getting back into his car and ramming them. But he remained perfectly still and mute.

"You're lucky we don't haul you in with your drug dealer friend, buddy! But we know where you live, so don't be surprised if you see us again real soon. Now get the hell out of here before I change my mind!" Charles obeyed. As he tiptoed his Honda away from the scene, he was sure he saw Stan's head pop up and peek out the back window as the cruiser sped away.

Chapter 31

Once Charles got back inside his house and locked the front door, he tried to sort out what had just occurred. He'd watched his best friend get brutalized by four cops for selling weed, and for playing hide-and-seek. Should he race right down to the station, try to bail him out? If they were going to jam him up on a "harboring a fugitive" rap, wouldn't they have done so at the scene?

Ding-ding. Stan on line one. Thank God. "Hey Charlie, sorry about all that. You think you can come down here and bail me out."

"Yeah, I'll be right there. But what about…"

"Don't worry. I told 'em I threatened you and carjacked your ass." Jesus, was he really laughing about this?

Driving over to the police station, Charles was more than a little worried that they might still try to jam him up for hiding Stan in his car. Just walking into the building made him uneasy.

"I'm here to post bail for Stanley Nowell."

"Name."

"Charles Smith."

"Have a seat, Mr. Smith. Someone will be right with you."

A few minutes later, a man poked his head and shoulders out of an office, pointed at Charles then wiggled his trigger finger in an unspoken order to "get over here."

"Mr. Smith. Your dope dealer pal gave us some bullshit story about carjacking you. We don't believe him, of course. You're lucky weed is practically legal these days. But you may want to be a little more selective about the people who choose to associate with, OK? This guy is bad news."

Yeah, I could tell by the way he went full Gandhi while your guys went all Rodney King on him that he's the one who's a menace to society. Beating the crap out of someone for selling a popular flower... you should be thankful he's not suing your department for using excessive force on a decorated Vietnam veteran.

Charles remembered Stan making some offhand comment about "medals," so he worked it into his imaginary lecture. As another officer led Stan around the corner, the first cop said, "OK, as soon as your friend here posts your bail, you're free to go. But we will be watching." Then he sneered, "See you in court... Apocalypse."

Back in the car, Stan was his usual self. "Wow, hell of a morning. We get in more scrapes with the Boys in Blue before 9 a.m. than most people get in all day. You wanna get high?" Stan produced a half joint—from whatever hiding place, Charles did not want to know—and lit it up before he could answer. Stan took a long puff and passed it over.

Why not? Charles thought to himself, as he pressed the thing to his lips and inhaled. The smoke lingered in his lungs as he held his breath for a moment, then it expanded and forced its way out, leaving him choking and Stan chuckling. "That's it, rookie. Cough to get off."

Charles soon pulled into his driveway and they went inside. Stan kept up the teasing, waving his fingers inches from Charles' face, pretending to conjure a trippy, psychedelic aura. "Don't start hallucinating on me now. I told you to stay away from that brown acid, Santana."

Charles was laughing now. Laughing at his friend's Woodstock joke. Laughing at how one of the bruises on his buddy's forehead reminded him of a Bugs Bunny cartoon. Laughing at Stan when he tried to keep a straight face while serenading Charles with a mangled Beatles lyric about "good Norwegian weed."

Laughing at just about everything now, their little run-in with the police seemed like fodder for a buddy sitcom or a lighthearted western—Beavis and Butt-Head meets Butch and Sundance. When "Helter Skelter" came on next, the two men went dead silent, staring at each other, expressionless—before losing it again. Hmm, Charles thought, smoking weed and cracking jokes with a friend really does have medicinal value.

Chapter 32

Next morning, Charles woke up a little foggy. He expected to find Stan snoring on the couch, but figured he must have walked home. When he staggered into the bathroom, Elmer wasn't at his usual spot on the mat in front of the shower. Charles brushed his teeth and headed for the kitchen to brew some coffee.

"Elmer?" said Charles.

"Meow."

"Meow," said Charles.

"Meeoooow."

He followed the sound to his back door and found the cat curled up between the recycling bin and some boxes. "Hey, you hungry?"

He went back to the kitchen, opened the fridge and tapped Elmer's spoon on the lip of the can. The cat took his time before appearing from around the corner. "What's the matter, little buddy?"

Elmer's normally squeaky meow was lower-pitched and elongated, and he kept twitching his head to the right, tapping but not quite scratching behind his ear with his right front paw. Charles grabbed him by the midsection, lifted him up and moved close to the sink for better light. He found a small wound there, leaking a little blood.

The cat's eyes were dilated, thick black pupils expanding wide into the hazel green of his irises. He didn't like being held upside down like this, and the black streaks that shaded the fur around his eyes made him look angry. He would occasionally sustain a little ding in the white area around his bright pink nose, Charles assumed from whatever he was up to in the dark. But this was different. He called the vet.

In the exam room, with Charles holding Elmer steady, Dr. Wood swabbed the area with a xylocaine jelly and began probing the wound. Within moments he had extracted a tiny metal bead. "It's a BB," said the vet. "Do you live in a wooded area?"

"No, he's an indoor cat." Charles squinted as he… No! He pictured the ringleader of the neighborhood pranksters out hunting birds and squirrels with a BB gun. Then he pictured him taking a shot at Elmer through the window overlooking the back stoop. If that little bastard shot his cat… Calm down for a second, he thought, let's get him home first.

After patching him up, the vet issued Elmer one of those upside-down lampshade devices to keep him from picking at the wound. He commented that the animal looked to be in excellent shape for a twelve-year-old that hadn't had a checkup since shortly after he was born. "It doesn't look like there's any serious damage. But if you notice any symptoms or after-effects, please get him back in here right away. Hopefully we won't need to order a CAT scan," said Dr. Wood. "That's a veterinarian joke, Mr. Smith."

Charles grimaced and thanked the vet, then crowded the cat back into his carrier and bolted for the exit. While whipping back home in the Honda, Charles reassured Elmer, "Don't you worry, buddy. Whoever did this to you is going to pay."

At home, Charles found the BB hole, right where he expected to. Elmer liked to sit on the sill of the window overlooking the tiny back yard, and that window had been shot through. Charles could see an area behind the chain-link fence where the shot probably came from— not exactly a grassy knoll, more like a tangled mess of overgrown shrubbery.

"OK, Bad Seed," Charles said, "you just brought a BB gun to a bazooka fight." Charles stepped outside and launched an empty orange flower pot against an unsuspecting tree. Then he channeled Samuel L. Jackson's character from *Pulp Fiction*, saying, "I will strike down upon thee with great vengeance and furious anger. And you will know my name is Charles Manson Smith when I lay my vengeance upon thee!"

There. That got it mostly out of his system for the moment. Now seething more calmly, he grabbed a small notebook and made himself a little memo. "W.A.R. Whiskey Alpha Romeo," he wrote. "This means war." He walked downstairs to the basement to poke around in his workshop.

Chapter 33

"Manson!" Charles wasn't sure how many scotches Quentin had in him, but he guessed at least a couple. "Goin' gangster! Harboring fugitives! What? You didn't think I'd hear about your little Mexican standoff with the *Federales*? I'm an ex-cop, man. I've got connections, scanners." Charles started to explain what happened, but Quentin cut him off.

"Pretty fuckin' hilarious. Plus, I think your buddy the Vietnam vet could make a great character for the book. Stanley 'Apocalypse' Nowell—you can't make that shit up."

Hmm, he couldn't argue with that. Maybe Apocalypse could help take down the villain, prevent some sort of global Armageddon. Actually, it was starting to seem like Quentin wanted the villain to win. Maybe Armageddon is the hero/villain. Dirk Armageddon. Charles definitely had a few clues, but Quentin's vision for this thing still felt like a big mystery.

"OK, I'm thinking this guy is part Michael Corleone, part Walter White, part Goldfinger and part Schwarzenegger, with a little Indiana Jones and a whole lotta Tony Montana."

"You mean the villain or the hero?"

"Villain. Hero. It all kind of blurs together these days, doesn't it."

Damn straight, thought Charles.

"OK, picture it. I'm seeing scorpions, Ebola, maybe some anthrax, helicopters, of course, countdowns, war rooms, a remote bunker in Oklahoma, AK-47s, 72 virgins, mustard gas, metal suitcases and mushroom clouds."

Wow! This guy may be nuts, but he'd probably kill in Hollywood. Charles tried to pick up the thread, continue the action-adventure-terror chain reaction.

"What if we throw in some box-cutters and bazookas, a Komodo dragon, polar icecaps, an albino, some alleged cannibalism, Putin, Pyongyang, and an unknown super-pathogen?"

"I like the way you think," said Quentin. "Hey, I've gotta take the Humvee down to the gym and beat the crap out of a sparring partner. It's raining out there. You wanna take the Jag?"

If by 'the Jag' you mean that sweet vintage Jaguar XJ12 I saw in your garage, then I say, fuck yes. Charles tried to mask his excitement, saying, "Are you sure you don't mind?"

The sports car rode a lot smoother than his tired old Civic. He liked seeing what the coastal route looked like with that iconic leaping Jaguar hood ornament in the foreground. Charles pretended he was rich as he rolled across causeways and bridges, past the Coast Guard station, the town common, the grand old resort hotel next to the marina—smiling all the way, waving to people he didn't even know. When he got home, he had to park a few doors down—within view of Mr. Ringleader's house.

This concerned him. The Bad Seed had already vandalized Charles' shitbox Civic. He feared that the Jaguar, its badass, big-cat hood trophy acting as a shiny punk magnet, could be an endangered species with that hoodlum on the prowl. Then an idea emerged—delicious, mildly maniacal, but certainly not fully unhinged or deranged. He hightailed it home to gather a few supplies.

Back at the car, he opened the hood. From an observer's point of view, it would appear he was checking a few cables, topping off the wiper fluid or just admiring its sick V12 engine. This was a complex piece of machinery, but Charles was handy with all manner of mechanical systems—even fancied himself a bit of a mad scientist, absent-minded professor type—so the operation didn't take long.

Satisfied, he reached up and used both hands to lower the hood and nudge it closed. Boy, that hood ornament was a beauty—front paws extended, jaw stretched open, sleek body uncoiled and ready to strike. As he polished it, he imagined that evil little bastard looking down from his bedroom window. And when he turned around he was almost certain he saw a curtain move on the second floor.

Later, Charles awoke in the wee hours to Elmer nudging his nose. Not his usual M.O., but not unusual either. The recently traumatized cat looked quizzical in his lampshade collar.

It was still dark outside as Charles spooned out some

breakfast shreds, then pulled on sweatpants and a flannel shirt to go check on the Jag. As he walked outside and approached the vehicle he could see the hood ornament, intact. But when he got closer a wave of terror tore through his soul. Lying near the car's front bumper was the kid, BB gun by his side.

Charles ran to him and kneeled over his lifeless body. "Hey kid!" Thank God, yes, there was a pulse. He was breathing too, but he seemed to be out cold. Charles grabbed his phone to punch in 9-1-1. Wait! He saw a rectangle in the kid's pocket, fished out his phone and made the call. "Help," he said, trying to camouflage his voice, "111 Gates Street."

He got behind the wheel, backed up a few feet and gassed it over to Quentin's house. He left the Jaguar in the driveway, tossed the keys on the seat and ran. Panic, revulsion, nausea. His medium-voltage booby trap had gone horribly haywire—and now all hell was breaking loose in his brain. The kid was comatose, maybe even dead. *It was an accident*, he testified under oath to himself, *an* accident. A gruesome, abominable freak fucking accident. In the distance, he could hear an ambulance. When Charles got home he went straight to the mirror to hate on himself.

You sick, soulless, subhuman fuck! Jesus, Manson, what have you done? His certainty that he had been cursed from birth had been with him for as long as he could remember. He was used to it. But *this*. The warped specter reflected in the glass appeared barren and transparent, anesthetized by its own noxious exhaust fumes—utterly, incurably damned. He knew that hell did not exist, but he also knew he was nine-tenths of the way there.

Charles thought about ways to end it all, right then and there. Self-imposed capital punishment, no appeal, no clemency. But he still didn't own a gun, he hated the smell of carbon monoxide in the morning, and wrist blood gave him the willies. *Gutless jellyfish. On the other hand*, he thought, looking over at Elmer eyeing him from the hallway, *fuck that little punk.*

Chapter 34

Eyes darting, Charles scanned the morning news on his laptop.

"Man pleads no contest to baseball bat attack…"

"Trial set in middle school sex assault case…"

"Gun sales surge after Concord school shooting…"

What a dark goddamn world we live in, he thought, *and New Hampshire is one of the nicest parts.* He continued panic-surfing the website of his old paper, searching for any news about the authorities reporting a mysterious incident on Gates Street.

"Maine man charged with robbing downtown bank…"

"City Council to hold hearing on helicopter noise…"

Yes, here it is.

Boy, 13, in serious condition

PORTSMOUTH—A Gates Street boy is in serious but stable condition today after EMTs responding to an early-morning 911 call rushed him to Coastal Hospital with unknown symptoms. Hospital

officials released no information about the nature
or cause of his condition. Police are investigating.

Charles' surge of relief that he was not, yet, guilty of
homicide or involuntary manslaughter (boyslaughter?)
was interrupted by a sharp knock at the door.

"Morning, sir. I'm Officer Goode and we're looking into
an incident that occurred a couple of hours ago just up the
street. Have you noticed anything unusual today?"

*You mean like a demented psychopath speeding away
from the scene in a Jaguar after nearly killing his child
nemesis with an electrical shock in some twisted revenge plot
for shooting his beloved cat with a BB gun?*

"No, officer. What's going on?"

"We're really not sure. A boy was found comatose
next to the curb. It appears he called 911, but he was
out cold when the EMTs got there. He's since regained
consciousness, but he's really fuzzy about what happened.
They're still doing tests."

Charles didn't know how to respond. *Oh my God?
That's shocking? I hope he's OK? Do they suspect foul play?*
If the officer was good at reading people, any answer that
sounded the slightest bit off might make him suspicious.
"Good luck. I hope he's OK," he finally said, shooting for
a monotone delivery and a blank expression. When the
door closed between them, Charles paced the room. He
had dismantled the mechanism from the Jaguar, and was
pretty sure he had not left any clues. Stupid tell-tale heart,
notwithstanding.

Suddenly, his novel was calling to him again; actually, more like shouting at him. This was not the first time in his life that a prank had backfired with catastrophic consequences. There was at least one incident that was scorched into his soul forever...

Charles thought he was being clever. Among the novelty items he'd ordered from his favorite catalog of gags—fake blood, snappy gum, itching powder—was a little tin of wooden sticks called "cigarette loads," presumably because when the prankster loads one into a cigarette, then stealthily slides it back into the pack, it delivers an explosive surprise just seconds after ignition.

The sketch accompanying the product in the catalog was undeniably hilarious—stout man in a 'wifebeater' T-shirt, a comically outraged expression plastered across his blackened, soot-covered face, his lips gripping a blown-up butt emitting a wisp of smoke. However, the makers and/or purveyors of the cigarette loads were somewhat negligent in failing to issue the following warning.

Caution: Using this product as intended may cause extreme rage and result in a beating so severe that the recipient winds up in the hospital for three days undergoing treatment for injuries including but not limited to: head bruises, subdural hematoma and third-degree burns.

But an eleven-year-old kid doesn't always

think things through when his mind is still discombobulated from the latest episode in an escalating pattern of paternal abuse and from watching his mom get knocked around the kitchen for alleged subpar preparation of twice-baked potatoes. Nor does he make the mental calculation that the prank's intended victim would not waste time "getting to the bottom of this" before erupting in a frenzy of backhands, forehands and fists. Or that two weeks later the four-figure hospital bill would trigger yet another, this time untreated, case of buttocks contusions.

Now nursing all these wounds, and more, Charles figured he had learned a valuable lesson about pranks. But had he?

The flashback was so visceral that he almost choked on the acrid clouds of tobacco that still smoldered in his mind—the memory so pungent that the bitter smog from his father's Viceroys wafted across the decades straight into his nostrils. Charles went into the bathroom and coughed up something black.

Again staring himself down in the mirror, Charles spit out a mouthful of toothpaste when his phone rang.

"So, anything you want to tell me?" Quentin asked.

Charles was sure he had returned the Jaguar in pristine condition, with no shred of evidence that it had ever been rigged to deliver a mild (it was supposed to be mild, medium at worst!) shock to a now-convalescing juvenile delinquent.

"Uh, no. Thanks for letting me use the Jaguar."

"Sure. Just wondering if anything weird went down in your neighborhood today?"

OK, Big Brother," Charles thought. *You tell me. What exactly do you know? And what do your pals down at the precinct think happened?*

"I guess they found some kid passed out by the curb," said Charles. "A cop filled me in while he was making the rounds asking people if they'd seen anything. Why, is there more to the story? What do your contacts say?"

"Under investigation. They've ruled out drugs. No external injuries. But the kid can barely speak. Detective said he felt like he was talking to a robot with a lobotomy."

"Wow. What do you think? Latest sign of the apocalypse? Paper said there was an attempted bank robbery, too. It's a jungle out there."

"Yeah," said Quentin. "I think there's something fishy about that case. Kid apparently was no choir boy."

Charles was finally starting to feel confident that Quentin was not on to him. So he decided to play him for more intel. "Maybe he had enemies. Pissed off the wrong people. What's on his rap sheet?"

"Mostly small-time stuff—vandalism, break-ins, shooting up animals. But he also cold-cocked another kid on the playground last month and before that he was accused of some inappropriate contact with a little girl."

"Jesus." Charles' gut was torn over what to feel. Thanks to him, this kid might never go to the prom, get married, have children. Or, thanks to him, the kid might never date rape a young woman, beat the shit out of his wife, abuse his children, kill somebody. "What else you hearing?"

"They've got specialists looking at him. But one of the neurologists told my guy he wasn't optimistic," Quentin said. "Hey, before we hang up — about my story. I'm starting to think this protagonist has deep-seeded psychological issues that inhibit his ability to distinguish between right from wrong."

Gulp.

Chapter 35

"You look like you seen a ghost."

Stan had just asked Charles about that kid, Josh Harper. Great, the boy had a name now. Bad Seed. Ringleader. Or just plain Josh. Yes, he had seen a ghost or three. He saw the apparition of a thirteen-year-old lying in a hospital bed giving him the finger. Then the specter of an older man—smoking, cursing and raising his hand to smack him. And the worst one of all, the one he caught regular glimpses of in the bathroom mirror.

"Hey, you losing weight, Stan?"

"Sure buddy, it's my new diet. T&A—twice a day."

Stan's laughter ripped into the room and echoed off the walls. Charles managed a chuckle, too. He loved when his friend popped over to visit unannounced. He was kind of like a Kramer character who'd inhaled a little too much Agent Orange. "You want a beer, Stan?"

"Got anything stronger?" Charles reached into the broken-knobbed cupboard above the fridge and pulled out an old bottle of Jameson's. "I was thinking tequila, but this'll definitely do." They clinked mismatched glasses as the conversation bounced back to the mysterious kid by the curb.

"Got any inside dirt?" asked Stan.

I could tell you Stan, but... Charles just shook his head, wishing he could confide in pretty much his only human friend about what happened and how it was accelerating his steady descent into darkness. Elmer came into the kitchen, making his midday rounds, and tilted his head up to greet Stan. "Hey, Elmer Smith. That's a good look for you, buddy. What happened?"

"Meow."

"He took a bullet to the back of the head, but I think it was meant for me," said Charles. Stan lost it again before stopping mid-laugh to give him a serious stare. "He got hit by a BB," said Charles, relieved that, at least in this case, he could just tell the truth without having to rewrite this part of his story. "You ever been shot, Stan?"

"Oh, hell yeah. Vietnam. Vegas too. Just missed me in Mexico." He pushed down on his belt and revealed a welt in the area near his right femoral artery. "Doc said if this one had been an inch and a half over I'd probably be dead. Two inches the other way," he shifted his hand so he was pointing directly at his groin, "and I'd wish I was."

Stan had been expecting a reaction, but Charles was quiet. "Hey, you OK?" he asked. "What's going on with your new ghostwriting job. Who is this character?"

Basically he's an ex-cop, ex-military egomaniac who wants me to help him write the Great American Terror

Novel. Definitely larger than life—two-dimensional, almost cartoonish, like a Batman or Bond villain," said Charles. "And get this, he owns the helicopter company that I hate. The other day he took me up on an aerial reconnaissance mission. His plot centers around a terror attack on the shipyard or the nuke plant."

"Whoa! Stop the presses there for a second. Did you say Quentin? You're not talking about a Lt. Roger Quentin are you?"

"Yeah, Lt. Roger Quentin. Lives over on Marcy Street."

"You do a background check on this guy?" Charles couldn't recall ever seeing Stan look so serious. "Actually, who knows what you'd find. It's probably hush-hush. I don't even know if the stories are true. But some of the guys in my unit used to talk about a Marine commander who lost his marbles and got discharged cause he kept talking about crashing a chopper into the fucking Pentagon. Quentin. I wouldn't forget that name."

Stan stood up and started to walk toward the kitchen. "You got any more of that whiskey?" He came back with the bottle, took a swig and then handed it to Charles. "Alright. Next time this Quentin character wants to take you up in his chopper, you gotta let me come with, OK?"

Charles smiled and nodded. "As a matter of fact, I don't think it's going to take a lot of convincing—and please sit back down on the edge of your seat as the plot thickens—because Lt. Roger Quentin, whoever he is, is very interested in you, my friend."

"Huh?"

"Oh, yeah. He third-degreed me about our alleged carjacking, dope-dealing adventure the other day. He brought up your name—I sure as hell didn't—and he said, quote, 'I think your buddy the Vietnam vet could make a great character for the book. Stanley Apocalypse Nowell— you can't make that shit up.' That's what he said."

Charles watched as Stan's face went from wide-eyed wonder to mischievous grin. "Well, I'll be goddamned to Satanville. Don't be too surprised if I make that whackjob son of a bitch regret the day he ever invited me into his book."

Chapter 36

The house fly Charles had waged war with was back—dive-bombing his head and shoulders, eluding his efforts to shoo and swat it away, as he walked to the post office. That it had taken on the appearance of a red helicopter did not seem odd to him. No sense in having midday delusions, he figured, if they weren't part of a relentless, richly textured conspiracy to drive oneself over the edge, right?

At moments like this Charles felt like a willing accomplice in his own inexorable unraveling, at once analyzing his psychological freefall from the side while also rushing headlong into it. Today it was the fly becoming a helicopter. Perhaps tomorrow he would metamorphize into the fly—like Jeff Goldblum, poor bastard—or better yet a cockroach, though hopefully a smaller one than Kafka's wretched beast.

Though Charles was annoyed that the fly was soiling the blue sky with noise pollution and despoiling his view of the magnificent church steeple and clock that marked time—minutes, hours, centuries—in the center of the town square, he was also transfixed, pausing to consider possible symbolism in the red light blinking near its rear rotor.

He held the door for an elderly woman. She nodded and offered a tired smile. But, was it just him, or did her eyes betray a certain sadness that suggested a fast-growing fear of her own mortality. Charles gave himself a gentle slap on his right cheek—a self-deprecating physical gesture he occasionally employed to disassociate himself from particularly engrossing episodes of introspection.

Dammit. He didn't see Keri Ann at the counter. Their Sunday bike ride had gone so well—way too well, for such a proactive pessimist as himself—that his strong desire to initiate a follow-up conversation had been impeded by his obsessive focus on calculating the risks of actually doing so. Now, having summoned the nerve to make a special trip to say hi—separated only by the four-foot-tall, three-foot-wide postal counter—his disappointment was assuaged by a mild sense of relief.

He walked over to his box, twisted his key in the lock and pulled out a wad of unsolicited rubbish—wastes of paper from an insurance company, home equity usurers and credit card exploiters, along with a fake check from a used car dealer. There was also something else lodged in the back, probably a five-by-eight flyer for the newest overpriced margarita joint or a $10 coupon for a lube-and-filter job. When he peeked into the box to grab the thing and toss it, a pair of familiar green eyes peered back at him—almost certainly a mirage manifested from nothing more than his feverish wishes to see her.

"Well hello there, Mr. P.O. Box 562."

Charles was pretty sure that the vision speaking to him from the other side of that tight, long, rectangular tunnel was an actual person—actually not a person, the person. "I, I came to see you, but…"

"I'm on box duty today," she said, always so buoyant, her easy manner diffusing most of his tension. "Getting a workout back here." Charles felt his forehead scrunch as he wracked his brain for the natural next thing a normal person might say. "Hey, you look super stressed," she said. "Have you ever tried yoga?"

No. "Yes." Of course, he had never tried yoga, could barely imagine trying to sit or stand still and wipe his mind clear of all the craziness. "Well, I go to the 7 a.m. class every Tuesday and Thursday at Body Sattva. You should stop by and check it out sometime."

"OK. I'll have to dust off my old mantra."

"You're thinking of transcendental meditation."

He wasn't. But in the search for something clever to say in the hope of making her smile, he had failed to bend either of the snippets of wordplay he was entertaining into a polished one-liner. At least the mantra quip saved him from blurting out something about "stop and smell the poses" or "it's a downward dog-eat-dog world out there." *Phew.*

"Oh yeah," he said. "I'll see you soon."

Several days later he showed up at the studio in his stupid gray sweatpants clutching his squishy, brand new yoga mat. Charles scanned the room trying to find Keri

Ann and spotted her in the back corner. He spread out his mat as close as to her as he could.

He had been sweating showing up at this session because he knew that anger and yoga did not mix. He felt relatively calm at the moment, but once things got under way there was an implied obligation to focus mindfully on the soothing words of the instructor—to banish one's troubles, tensions and distractions; to simply let go of the aberrant daydreams, the neurotic hysteria and the schizo-affective personality disorders that we come to take for granted in our everyday lives. But these were some of the very things that helped Charles keep his head on straight and he feared that monkeying around with that loosely hinged, dysfunctional Rube Goldberg contraption could trigger the mother or all meltdowns.

As soon as the class began, his mind raced rather than slowed, and he had the sensation that he was being ordered to relax. He tried to drift into the experience but soon became caught up in one of his absurdist flights of fancy. "Slowly lie down. Stretch out your hands. Now stretch your feet. Reeelaaax and just breeeeaaathe." For some reason, the instructor's whispery intonations, which seemed to pacify the other participants, felt aggressive to Charles. He began to imagine the yoga instructor morphing into a yoga drill instructor—Sgt. Namaste.

"Drop and give me 20 savasanas, you sniveling little maggots!"

"I said hit the floor! You DID not come here at oh-seven-hundred hours to suck your thumb and daydream about *nirvana, you meatless sacks of tofu! I said assume the position! Your inner peace is not going to find itself!"*

Then the imaginary drill instructor marched forward and got right up in Charles' face, approximately an inch from his nose.

"You are a lean, mean relaxation machine! Do you hear me!?"

"Sir! Yes, sir!"

Charles gasped and tried to inhale his words, but it was too late.

"Charles!" Keri Ann was looking at him like he was some kind of lunatic. "Uh... Uh... I was picturing..." He was trembling and she did not understand why. His eyes looked intense, stormy. She could feel his distress. "Do you want some water?"

When she handed him the bottle, Charles noticed a light smudge of lipstick around the rim. He touched the bottle to his lips before taking a sip. Finally, he exhaled and spoke one word before turning and fleeing the scene. "Namaste?"

Chapter 37

Charles grabbed his laptop, not sure if he was going to bang out a chapter in his own book or officially get started on Quentin's. But first things first. Nope, Google turned up zero on Quentin's alleged Section 8.

He had some hazy recollections of his father talking about Vietnam—mostly hateful drivel about wishing he could have gone there to kill some "gooks" or about wanting to bash in the heads of some anti-war "hippies." The man hated Kennedy, liked LBJ and loved Nixon, but turned sour on him after his historic diplomatic mission to visit "the chinks." Big Archie Bunker fan, too. Hateful dumbass—too stupid to understand the joke was on him. Charles was more of a *M*A*S*H* man. He loved the rapid-fire satire, how the writers shot from the hip and aimed for the heart, always portraying the warmongers as assholes. He made a mental note to try to think of that theme song the next time he heard the sound of a chopper. Then his fingers started moving.

The school bus had stopped. The lights were

flashing. The driver pulled his handle to open the door. But Charles didn't budge. "Hey, Speed Racer. You getting off?" The driver called him Speed Racer because of his lunch box.

Charles trudged down the school bus steps and across Turner Road to the ranch-style home with the big front yard where he and his brother sometimes pretended they were cheetahs—sleek, spotted big cats racing from one thicket of trees to the other. Today, the report card in his hand would surely earn him a thrashing. His dad would not even notice the A's in English, Math, Social Studies and Science, not once he laid eyes on the bottom line. Physical Education: D+.

His father hated the fact that he preferred books and intellectual pursuits to athletics—probably couldn't stand having a kid who could think him under the table. "Put down that fucking Hardy Boys bullshit and go outside and play baseball like a normal kid," his father would bellow, on a good day. But if he was drunk, he would just cuff him on the back of the head, knock whatever he was reading out of his hands and say it was time for another "boxing lesson." No gloves. Mostly slapping, but slipping some fist work in too.

Jab-jab-cross. Jab-cross-left uppercut-cross. "Get up."

Right cross-left hook-right cross. "Fight like a man, little girl."

On this particular day he tried to slip the report card to his mom, but his father snatched it and set his beer down on the counter. "It's report card day, right? Let's have a look." When the man's eyes narrowed and his jaw tightened, Charles braced himself for the usual combo. Verbal abuse to the brain—bam! Physical beating to the body—boom!

"Jesus Christ! D+... What did I tell you. You sissy-ass bookworm. Boxing lesson—put up your fucking hands!"

"Richard!" cried his mom.

"I'll give you some too," his father shouted.

Snapping back to reality, Charles was even angrier at himself than usual—pissed off that his never-ending flashbacks could still make him feel gutless and weak. He slapped shut the cover of his laptop and fired it hard into the couch, cursing himself as it bounced onto the floor. Then he grabbed a pillow, pressed it tight to his face and screamed. He slipped on his Skechers and headed out to do a little shopping.

OK, mission accomplished. Charles felt emboldened by the extra twenty-seven ounces that now hung in a holster just below his left shoulder. He'd known it was only a matter of time before he'd go back to the gun store to pick up a small pistol. He liked the shape, the look, the feel, even the name of the 9 mm Beretta Px4 Storm Subcompact. At 6.2 inches long with a 3-inch barrel, 4.8 inches high and 1.4 inches thick, he figured it would do the job—whatever the job might end up being.

Driving home, he started to squirm a bit at the idea that strapped to his chest several inches from his heart was a mechanism that could easily kill him if he failed to exercise extreme caution. He imagined standing his ground, neutralizing a threat, maybe wasting a lowlife in self-defense. Home invasion? *Go ahead, make my day.* Pop! Pop! Pop! *Are you threatening me? We deal in lead, friend.*

He didn't have any particular short-term plans to draw down, start blasting and put somebody six feet under in a pine box. But one never knew what sort of blood-drenched firefight unexpected hostilities might trigger. "Better to have a gun and not to need it than to need a gun and not to have it," said President Theodore Roosevelt. Or was it Samuel L. Jackson.

Anyway, it's like the National Rifle Association says: "The only thing that stops a bad guy with a gun..." here he edited himself into the NRA rhetoric, "is a badass motherfucker with a Beretta Px4, bitch." If anyone tried to get hold of his gun, thought Charles, they'd have to take it from his cold, dead hands. He got home, stripped off his holster and locked the goddamn thing in his safe.

Chapter 38

"The Madman Cometh."

"What?"

"Slaughterhouse Now."

"Jesus. What are you talking about?"

Quentin's eyes looked glazed but wild. He was marching around his office slapping items of furniture for emphasis.

"Red Badge of Death. Gentlemen Prefer Bombs. I'm looking for book titles, Ghostie," he said, trying out a new nickname for his ghostwriter. "I've been up all night thinking up names for the book."

Charles liked the idea of tweaking a classic title into something that would resonate in the collective public consciousness and also demand attention. But at this stage he also thought it might make a little more sense to, you know, rough out the plot and flesh out the central characters. But there was no sense in interrupting the man until he burned himself out. Plus, his bizarre stream of consciousness might give Charles some insight into his mind and what kind of story it was trying to tell.

"Lord of the Skies. Rebel Without a Conscience. Planes, Trains, and Helicopters…"

"Raging Bullets. Depraved New World. One Flew Over the Eagle's Nest…"

"Mr. Smith Blows Up Washington."

Definitely not a big Uncle Sam fan, got it.

"We the Puppets. Detonation of Independence."

Yep.

"Farewell to the Arms Race. The Sun Also Burns—Ernie Hemingway, baby!"

Thank you, muscular Hemingway-esque prose was already on the list.

"Cannibals. Something about cannibals as a metaphor for mankind eating his own flesh, then crapping it out and eating the crap for dessert," he barked. *Well, now that's dark and demented,* thought Charles. *Have you considered that a mental illness subplot might be seeking expression in this 'novel' of yours?*

"And torture," said Quentin, pausing to catch his breath. "Any terror book worth its salt has got to have torture. Terror and torture go together like fire and brimstones."

Charles studied the notes on his laptop then launched into a ponderous query urging Quentin to offer some reflection regarding whether any elements of his story—or indeed the central thrust of this frenzied nuclear-themed terror odyssey with apocalyptic overtones—might in any way be animated by his apparent anti-government animus, specifically whether there were any incidents or experiences in his own life potentially fueling his desire to unleash a tsunami of hellfire down upon America as we know it. But when he looked up to gauge his response, the man's head had slumped down onto his right shoulder. As he began snoring, Charles could have sworn he heard him mutter the word, "tsunami."

Quentin seemed to be sound asleep, so Charles got up to do some quick snooping while he snoozed. Creeping up to the wide, heavy wooden desk, he noticed some maps, a helicopter manual and some notes and sketches on a yellow legal pad. Most of the pencil marks looked like the scrawlings of crazy person. The man clearly had no skill for drawing mushroom clouds.

He leaned closer and noticed that Quentin was wearing a shoulder holster containing a handgun about twice as big as Charles's own Beretta. Other items on the desk included some powdery black residue, several receipts from East Coast Aviation Fuel and an official-looking document that appeared to be a will. He started reading: "I, Roger T. Quentin, being of sound mind and rational thought, willfully and voluntarily..." But Quentin's snore turned into a grumble and he opened his eyes.

"So yeah, those were some heavy book title ideas you were dropping just now," said Charles. "I was thinking we should go up for another brainstorming flight. And, uh, my friend Stan mentioned he'd love to ride along."

"Hell yeah, love to meet him," said Quentin, rubbing his right hand up over his face and back down. "Tell me more about Apocalypse Nowell."

"Ex-Marine. Badass biker type. Lots of tattoos.

Tradesman, handyman. Pretty much retired. You already know about his alleged side business as a cannabis entrepreneur." Charles did not mention that his friend flew choppers while serving in Vietnam. He also left out the part where Stan raised the possibility that the aspiring ex-cop novelist might be a certified psycho who was plotting an actual domestic terror attack instead of just writing a book about one.

Leaving Quentin's house, Charles couldn't wait to tell Stan he had scheduled him for a chopper ride. So he was thrilled to see his friend's leather-bagged Harley parked on his lawn.

"Hey! We're on for next Tuesday," he shouted. "High noon."

"Fantastic," said Stan. "What's that, the 11th?"

"Yeah, I guess." Charles also filled Stan in on Quentin's increasingly erratic behavior, the drawings, the will, the jet fuel receipts, the gun. Stan squinted his right eye and pointed at him. "You think he's up to something, right?"

Probably, Charles thought. *But when it comes to offering rational, objective assessments about the difference between someone who is engaging in wildly imaginative, violent fantasies and someone who is actually on the brink of snapping and causing serious harm to himself and/or others, I'm not always the best person to ask.*

"Hard to say. But Quentin sure is looking forward to meeting you."

"One way to deal with guys like that is to taunt them," said Stan.

"What do you mean?"

"Hard to explain. You'll see." Charles trusted Stan, but it occurred to him that this cryptic "taunt the psychopath" philosophy might have the potential to backfire. Well, Charles had already decided to pack the Beretta for their little field trip.

"Hey, did you see? The news this morning had a report about that kid they found by the curb. Apparently he still hasn't said a word; they're not sure he ever will. But you'll never guess what they found out."

Charles felt the room go dark and the walls start to collapse inward.

His guilt felt like quicksand—thick, heavy and slowly engulfing him. He was certain it would shorten his life and felt he surely deserved some form of punishment, whether administered by society, himself or whatever omniscient supreme being may or may not be observing this shithole world from its (his, her, their?) billowy, celestial cloud perch.

"His folks let the cops search his room and nose around the house for clues about what might have happened, and they found some pretty mind-blowing shit. Turns out the kid was some kind of cat and dog serial killer."

"Very funny, Stan."

"I swear to God." Stan raised his right hand and continued. "The little psycho apparently kept this scrapbook filled with posters of missing pets that their owners put up in the neighborhood, and it led them to a burying ground in his back yard. Said they dug up more than a dozen. It's like something out of a Stephen King book." Stan paused and his bewildered stare cut through Charles' skepticism. He was serious.

"Scrapbook had little, like, book reports on Bundy, Dahmer, Son of Sam, the Beantown Strangler, Jack the Ripper. Manson too. I mean they stopped just short of saying the kid was a future John Wayne Gacy in the making." Charles remained mum, stunned, as he struggled to process what he was hearing, waiting to see if Stan had more to say. "The parents are freaked out. Report said they'd be shipping the kid to some psychiatric hospital."

"McLean?"

"Yeah, maybe. Holy shit though, right?" Charles just nodded, feeling blessed that Elmer was not among the victims.

Chapter 39

"OK, we need to get serious." Terror, anarchy, death choppers and mushroom clouds were all well and good, but Charles felt he needed to get Quentin focused on the nuts and bolts of his novel—the actual story, the protagonist and supporting characters, the setting, the plot.

"Your protagonist," he said. "Just who is this guy and what is his motivation?"

"OK." Quentin just stared at him for at least 20 seconds before unleashing a stream-of-consciousness brain dump. "I guess you could say this guy—Quentin Blood, Buck Ulysses, Benedict Armageddon, whatever we end up calling him—is loosely based on me.

"He's an ex-Marine in incredible physical condition— fast, strong, tough as nails, ripped like Rambo. Plus he's a genius. We're talking Sherlock Holmes, da Vinci, Hannibal Lecter-level intellect. He's got some mad scientist in him—definite MacGyver vibe, but with a sinister edge. But he's also got issues, and I don't just mean cocaine and kamikazes, shaken not stirred. He's troubled, maybe even a little unhinged. He bangs a lot of gorgeous women, some of them spies, but also supermodels, actresses, princesses, champagne sommeliers, Miss Universe contestants, hot librarians, nurses and bartenders. But he doesn't let that distract him from his mission."

"Which is…"

"Don't worry, it's not some hackneyed world domination bullshit. This guy's a patriot. But also an ex-patriot and an anti-patriot. He's a humanist who feels he's been dehumanized, screwed over by his own country, booted from the Marines after reading the Pentagon Papers made him want to blow up the Pentagon.

"He believes the Founding Fathers would be ashamed that today's chicken-hawk government blasted into Iraq over fake weapons of mass destruction to funnel trillions of taxpayer dollars to their military-industrial pals, that they tap our phones and read our emails, feed Wall Street greed and kick corporate welfare back to Big Oil and Big Pharma while keeping we the people hooked on petrochemicals and other poisons.

"He decides he wants to send some kind of a message, rather than just wait around for Washington to do the next horrible, hypocritical, self-serving thing. So he buys, steals and invents as many weapons as he can get his hands on, starts writing an epic manifesto and making plans to go postal. Maybe he rewires some NASA rockets to launch World War III. Or maybe he just gets fed up and flies a helicopter into a federal building.

"By the end of the book—against the backdrop of an

apocalyptic orange, white and blue inferno—you see his burnt-up skeleton straddling a sidewinder missile and laughing all the way to hell. Lt. Strangelove meets Citizen Fahrenheit. Boom. The End."

Charles didn't know whether to call Coppola, the cops or the FBI—metaphorically speaking, of course. The FBI was out of the question. People who were already on the Bureau's watch list and had recently fried the brain of an alleged future serial killer should try to keep a low profile. Plus, he had zero proof that Quentin was anything other than a highly creative, raving lunatic.

"Hmm," he said, "sounds like you've really been giving this a lot of thought. This is very helpful. For our next session, I want you to drill down on the plot. Let's figure out what's really going on here."

After pulling Quentin's front door closed behind him, Charles found himself paying closer attention to his gait as he made his way to the post office. His strides felt looser and longer, his mental footprint less cumbersome than the day before.

Inside, he liked to hang back near the window, next to one of the high tables where people sorted and discarded their mail, to observe Keri Ann's interaction with her customers. She probably wondered why he hadn't called or stopped by since that craziness at the yoga studio. As she finished up with an elderly African-American gentleman who looked to be in his mid-60s, he noticed how the man's world-weary expression brightened in response to her smile.

"Good to see you, Mr. Washburn," she said. "Glad to hear the hip is feeling better."

"God bless you, dear," he said, and then whispered, "Obamacare."

The next man in line, a chunky, small-eyed white fellow wearing a Crimson Tide polo shirt, huffed and spit out the words, "Obama. Friggin' monkey-ass (n-word)." Charles took a step forward then paused. He felt a distinct twitch, as if a light bulb had fizzled and popped in his head, then blinked back on, brighter and hotter than before. He wondered if his brain had just blown a circuit breaker.

He aimed his eyes at the man's face and shook his head several times from right to left. Then he said—out loud, throwing in a couple extra decibels for emphasis—"No."

The man squinted at him and cocked his head.

"Not today," said Charles, even louder this time.

"What's your problem, pal. Don't believe in freedom of speech?"

"What do you say you and I walk outside and have a little First Amendment debate," said Charles, now glaring at the man—mind wired, muscles tensed. "Either that, or you can apologize to Mr. Washburn here and everybody in this room. Right now."

The man fell silent and his eyes dropped to the floor. "Fuck this. Uh. Sorry." He pulled his Redskins cap further down on his forehead, snuck another glance at Charles and bolted for the door.

Though still in the throes of an out-of-body experience— behind the hazy translucent veil that shielded his impaired yet hyper-lucid private universe from the hopelessly problematic external world—Charles was peripherally aware of a buzz permeating the lobby. He felt a hand on his shoulder.

"Bless you, son," said Everett Washburn. "Pretty intense there, but it sure is good to see someone stand up for what's right."

"Sir," Charles nodded in acknowledgment, now feeling extremely self-conscious that he had actually vocalized some thoughts that he would normally lock down and internalize.

Now he noticed Keri Ann, glancing, then again, as she tended to the next customer. Her smile, the way she was looking at him, made him feel proud, even vaguely noble. He could barely imagine what he might say to her though, so he gave a nervous wave and walked away. He liked her so much. He thought he might even love her, but... But etched in his mind was that old saying that you need to love yourself before you can love someone else. And, well, Charles had long since resigned himself to the fact that the first part of that equation was just not going to happen.

Chapter 40

"Why the fuck am I here?" Charles had gotten up in the middle of the night to take a piss, and was trying to figure out why, instead of going right back to bed, he had walked into the kitchen.

Oh yeah, heartburn and a pounding headache. He swallowed some pills and started back to bed, where sleep—except for his thrice-weekly nightmares—was his only true refuge from the internal electrical storms that buffeted him through most of his waking hours. In the darkness, he could see a little orange light flickering on the power cord connected to his laptop. He walked toward it and mashed his left foot into the leg of the thick, low butcher-block table in front of the couch.

"Father-fucking son of a bitch!" His anger was so intense, it took him a split second to realize that his impulse to kick the table with his right foot would be a genius move to double the pain. Instead, he smacked the tabletop hard with his open hand and tried to let the rage flow from his body as the stinging in his hand teamed with the throbbing in his foot.

A moment later he was on the couch with his laptop. His headache was forgotten and so was the heartburn. He wished he was inspired to write about something other than morbid flashbacks mired in brooding self-scrutiny, but that's what kept coming out. He figured he'd have to work through it to find the real story, if there was one. And he was gradually feeling more certain that his bad daddy complex was more than just some weak-willed, woe-is-me bullshit. There was power in it.

He knew the man had broken him, even before his earliest, horrible memories. Mother vs. father. Nurture vs. torture. One parent determined to raise the boy, the other trying to bury him. He wondered if the writing was a subconscious effort to raze the past and rebuild a future. If so, he doubted it would work. Damage done. The father had won.

It started out as one of the happiest days of his life.

Charles, a freshman, had won a writing contest for a humor piece about a baby with superhuman powers. It was published in the high school newspaper and the girl he secretly liked, a sophomore, not only said she enjoyed his story, she gave him a little kiss on the cheek.

But when you're a boy named Charles Manson Smith—walking joke, born loser—any tale that starts out "Boy meets girl, girl kisses boy" is doomed to devolve into: "Girl's jock brother beats up boy, gives boy a stars and stripes wedgie (clips boy's underpants to flagpole rope and yanks him off the ground), boy's father comes to school and further humiliates him in front of girl."

Sitting in the front seat on the way home, his father bawling him out for making him miss an hour of work and for being the world's all-time biggest failure, Charles was overwhelmed with desire to hurt both himself and the old man. So, about a mile from their turnoff on Route 8, he grabbed the steering wheel and tried to veer their station wagon into an oncoming dump truck. But the car sideswiped the truck and rammed into a bridge abutment. His head bloodied from slamming the windshield, he ran from the scene and kept running.

He spent that night curled in the corner of an abandoned junk-strewn cabin deep in the woods behind their house and the next night in a neighbor kid's tree fort. But in the morning the kid's mom called his mom. When he got home his dad thrashed him with his own Hot Wheels track and threatened to send him off to "the funny farm."

The creator of the baby with the superpowers felt utterly powerless, helpless and empty—stripped of everything but his anger, as if hanging half-naked from a flagpole for all to see.

Good lord. OK, it felt somewhat cathartic to put those words on paper—even made him feel for a moment that he might have the potential to contribute something meaningful as a writer. But he was also starting to question whether the answer to "what is the meaning of my life?" would be found by anguishing, in middle age, over a lost-boy confessional or helping a possible domestic terrorist pen a memoir/manifesto. He closed his laptop and fell asleep on the couch.

"Hi Keri Ann. You look lovely today as always."

"Why, thank you, Charles."

"Would you like to go the movies this Saturday and see that new romantic comedy where the troubled guy and the lovely woman overcome some sort of challenge then fall in love and live happily ever after?"

"That sounds wonderful," she said… her last words before the morning sun awakened him from his latest Keri Ann night dream.

This was the type of normal exchange he wished he could have with Keri Ann. Sure, the opening line was a little too Eddie Haskell. But not too bad for someone who—when wracking his brain to initiate a conversation with something that sounded natural and not at least partly insane—was more likely to instead, and in fact did last week, just blurt out… "Do you like cats?"

Fortunately, she did. He knew she would. She explained that she and her ex had adopted one at Christmastime, named her Bailey because they were sipping Bailey's after they brought her home. Charles pictured their two cats becoming best friends, soul-pets even, sharing the small rattling balls and fuzzy faux mice that were forever strewn about his floors. He could still barely talk to her, but at least he'd been able to put some of his feelings for her into a letter.

Alright, focus up. Today should be interesting, he thought. Heading into the skies to get another look at his city from above, and perhaps see some fireworks between Stan and Quentin. The downtown streets were crowded with tourists as he walked through Market Square down toward the pond, trying to remember exactly where he had parked his car.

He flinched as the bell in the North Church steeple— loud and looming almost directly above him—hammered out the first of 11 resonant clangs. He counted them off.

Two. A small dog was yapping its head off in a lady's purse nearby. He prayed for it to just shut up.

Three. A fat asshole threw a cigar butt on the ground in front of the coffee shop and a small boy reached to pick it up as his mother swatted at his hand to stop him. Charles wanted to throttle the man.

Four. A helicopter charged into the sky overhead, its rhythmic roar feeling so close to his ears that Charles ducked and wondered which was more common, being struck by lightning or decapitated by a chopper.

Five. He thought about the gun he was carrying today, assessing how self-conscious he felt walking around in public with a lethal weapon strapped to his ribs. The answer: extremely.

Six. Maybe he was just low on magnesium or iron or calcium or zinc or folic acid or omega-3 or sleep, but routine self-monitoring of his normally high level of agitation revealed that the needle was well into the red zone.

Seven. Perhaps his serotonin levels were being compromised by unusual activity involving norepinephrine and dopamine. Possible hypoglycemic imbalance involving glucose or gluten.

Eight. At least he could rule out lysergic acid diethylamide.

Nine. A biker's boot kick-starting an old Harley ruptured the air to his right.

Ten. A bagpiper let loose a shrill, reedy drone and began wailing from the other side of the square, suffocating him like a thick, cloying vapor. He felt at once mesmerized and antagonized, as if he should be stomping into battle or marching off a cliff.

Eleven: It reminded him of watching a long-ago parade—his father slapping him on the head to take off his hat, digging a fist into his spine then wrenching back his shoulders to stand him straight, yanking his arm and smashing his right hand onto his hard-thumping heart.

Still wired when he reached his Honda, he clicked his key to unlock the door and slid behind the wheel. He moved his right hand to check the bulge under his opposite shoulder, then recoiled as he touched it. Ignition. Turn signal. Pop it in drive. Pull out and accelerate. About a half-mile up the road he began to calm down. He gunned the engine toward the traffic circle on his way to meet Stan and Quentin at the airfield.

Chapter 41

As soon as he got to the circle, Charles filled the inside of the Civic with a storm cloud of expletives. Traffic was pushing back to where a flagman stood next to a line of orange cones. He let loose a primal scream and pounded three times on the steering wheel, then cursed the sun for bursting through the clouds and aggravating his eyes—his windshield visor long since missing in action, innocent casualty of some previous cabin pressure meltdown.

Cars jammed together impeding his progress always made Charles apoplectic. Plenty of hate to go around—too many vehicles crammed onto the road, every driver ahead of him making it worse by being a moron with butt flesh for brains.

Really, there were too many goddamn people on the planet—irrefutable mathematical fact. At times like this, even though he didn't actually wish for a plague to wipe millions of people off the face of the earth, in the privacy of his own car he did allow himself to ease the tension by wondering or uttering out loud such sentiments as "where's pestilence when you need it?" Pestilence alone wouldn't do the trick, of course, you also need famine, war, mortar fire—mortar and pestilence.

He was endlessly fascinated by the vast array of colorfully named, microscopic entities capable of bringing down fully grown humans by the thousands. Ebola and West Nile, EEE and SARS; bird flu, swine flu, mad cow and monkey pox. He pictured hundreds of mad cows being herded into anger management counseling. Death, death, death. Just a simple fact of life.

Fifty feet closer, Charles was back to thinking about Quentin. Creep ahead, forget to pay attention, slam on the brakes. He sensed the guy was one step ahead of him, probably even toying with him somehow. Ego junkies like him loved to jerk people around, pull strings and play games. Perhaps once they were aloft in the helicopter, the clouds would fade and the aerial perspective would yield more clarity.

Traffic eased for a second. Hey, another six inches. Charles edged closer to his escape valve, the exit where two cop cars bracketed a bulldozer surrounded by a dozen or so hard hats talking about—what?—the intoxicating scent of bituminous pavement? The Patriots?

Calculating that he still had plenty of time for a three- to four-minute flashback, Charles sank back in his seat and pictured himself on his very first plane ride, buckled in next to his mom and brother for the flight to California, seatbacks in the upright position. He remembered feeling vaguely uneasy, but thrilled to be putting a blast of jet engines and more than three thousand miles between himself and... himself. He wondered what the meal would be, what his new life would be like. Tap, tap, tap. What? A cop glowered into his window and waved him on his way.

The change of scenery and Pacific ambiance worked for a while, he recalled, churning up the past as he continued on toward the airfield. He clicked open the dictation app on his phone and let some memories flow. But young Charles soon discovered what he already dreaded and deep down knew, that his dad had planted the seed—both biologically and through his cruel brand of parenting—for a lifetime of misery and self-persecution.

And it blossomed out west, where he would be tossed out of several Bay Area schools—a "bright kid," breaking rules. After a series of mishaps involving misfiring fireworks, wine-country rabble-rousing, black eyes and bloody noses (mostly his), crumpled automobiles and a missing houseboat—not to mention getting dinged by Candlestick Park security for dashing onto the field in a Reagan mask and embarking on a psychedelic Hollywood road trip that resulted in significant memory loss and a bit part in the indie film "Follow the Monkey"—Charles didn't need any experts to tell him there was a pattern of troubling behavior.

Only by harnessing the manic delirium side of his personality to produce a trilogy of short stories described by a noted Beat Generation scholar as "unshaven skull-scorching psychedelic post-hipster pyrotechnics" was he fortunate enough to weasel into Stanford on a Stegner

Fellowship. Oh well, almost there. He'd have to reflect on how his college experience imploded another time.

As he neared the airfield, Charles could see Stan and Quentin up ahead standing next to a red chopper, engaged in conversation. They turned and greeted him with broad smiles and a flurry of arm gestures. "Ghostie," yelled Quentin. "Hey, your secret's out. Apocalypse here tells me you're writing two books. Just make sure mine is the bigger blockbuster."

"Don't worry," he said. "Yours is definitely larger than life. Larger than death. Maybe even larger than both." Quentin laughed loud and hard, as Stan chimed in and Charles managed to muscle out a chuckle.

"Yes!" Quentin put his fists together in front of his chin, then thrust his arms wide, spread his fingers and pursed his lips while exhaling as if to suggest an explosion. "Ba-boom!" he said, followed by another blast of seismic laughter as Charles and Stan glanced at each other.

"Well, gentlemen. I recommend you grab a headset and say your prayers, cause it's time to get this party started."

"I got shotgun," shouted Stan.

Chapter 42

As the helicopter's skids broke contact with the tarmac, the excitement got the best of Stan. "Whooooo! I ain't been up in one of these since '72."

"Bap-bap-bap-bap-bap." Now he was waving an imaginary machine gun to strafe an imaginary enemy on the ground below, his shoulders and torso actually shuddering as they absorbed the impact of the make-believe weapon. Quentin was loving the enthusiasm. "Hey, you missed a couple," he said, laughing. "I just saw a couple VC run behind that shed."

"Bap-bap-bap-bap-bap."

Quentin grabbed a pretend grenade, pulled the pin with his teeth and tossed it. "Die, you commie scumbags!"

Charles felt calm. He watched a trio of deer lope from a grassy area near the pavement into a grove of trees. There was a lot of wildlife out at the airfield and surrounding business park, the site of a former Air Force base. As the ground got smaller, he examined the familiar landmarks near the headquarters of his former newspaper—the water tank, the brewery, the National Guard base, digital companies doing business in older buildings next to the girdered frames of new ones sprouting up from the soil.

"Hey, isn't that where you used to work, before they laid your ass off?" Quentin was pointing to the wide two-story building that housed the Portsmouth Beacon, its now sparsely populated newsroom and business offices, and the presses.

"Yep." Charles remembered the first day he set foot in the Beacon's newsroom, back when it was located in a historic brick building downtown. The old Englishman who would become his mentor said, "I've been hearing good things about you," as Charles braced for some mention of the negative biographical information to which this gentlemen journalist surely also had access. Though he had long lamented squandering the potential he was told he had to become an "important" writer, Charles quickly came to feel an immense sense of pride in the work he was doing to keep several thousand readers informed about life in their community.

Almost as soon as he started there as a reporter, he was sent to a press conference at the Air Force base. Congress was making moves to trim the defense budget by closing unneeded military installations, but everyone knew that this base—a vital cog in the local economy and an essential national defense installation—was not on the list. But everyone was wrong. And the news hit the community like an old B-47 bombshell. Charles wrote about the base and the impact of its closure and renaissance for the next two decades, even taking road trips to northern Maine, upstate New York and the Midwest to report on other communities where the "peace dividend" had triggered hard times on the home front.

After a while, he was allowed to start writing columns and he tried to bring something special to his often-humorous tales of a historic town finding its way in the high-tech age. He felt blessed to visit fishing boats and lighthouses, to ride along on a snowplow in a Nor'easter, to interview storekeepers and lobstermen, cops and alleged robbers, historians, presidential candidates working the campaign trail and soldiers deploying to the desert—even a human cannonball.

Behind the scenes, sure, he was still a stoic ten-count away from snapping at any given moment, but the job helped him keep his grip—eight-plus-hour stretches that required him to maintain the appearance of sanity being one of the few job requirements. That incentive now stripped away, Charles felt unmoored but also energized. He could never deny that his wild moods and "me against them, me against me" feuds, though psychologically crippling, certainly came with an adrenaline-like dark euphoria that he found intoxicating.

Now the chopper was humming along the river. Below, he watched as a tall, muscular crane dipped its claws into the hold of a massive cargo tanker from some faraway port, filled the jaw of its hinged, hanging shovel, then swung the bucket over to a mountain of dirty brown road salt and let the minerals sift down onto the pile—the sandy, smoothness of the crane's delivery system reminding him of an hourglass.

Ahead he could see the Memorial Bridge. A tribute to the men and women who served—dating to post-World War I, then recently scrapped and rebuilt—its flat gray coloration and low-slung structure evoking images of a battleship. Though the tugboats and lobster vessels looked tiny from his perch, he could see a fisherman hauling up traps, removing his catch, replenishing the bait then dumping them back into the river. This kind of rugged, beautifully choreographed work—the poetic motions of the tugs and lobster boats; the tankers, cranes and Tonka trucks of the salt pile—he found mesmerizing.

"Ground control to Major Chuck. How you doin' back there, Space Cadet?" Quentin was pushing his buttons again and he felt himself getting irritated. "You're missing all the action." Quentin pointed inland toward the square, where it appeared that several police cars had gathered near the post office, blue lights set on strobe.

"Hey," Stan said to Quentin. "Charlie's been telling me about this novel of yours. I never been much of a book man, so I'll probably hold out for the movie version. But it sounds really wild." Quentin seemed pleased as he lifted the chopper to a higher elevation. "I know how that guy feels, man. Military vet, served his country, fought for freedom. You wanna be a righteous patriotic American," Stan said, tapping his fist two times on his heart. "But the government does some pretty sick shit." Quentin was nodding.

"I mean after 9/11 they let Osama get away to go chase down Saddam. Then Bush does a video making jokes about not finding the phony 'weapons of mass destruction.' Gotta tell you, brother, as a vet who lost friends in battle, that was fucking disgusting. Then they turn around and use terrorism as an excuse to spy on us back home. Tell me what kind of gun I can have. I can really see where some of these militia, survivalist assholes are coming from."

Stan must have practiced his rant, but Charles could tell that at least some of it was sincere. "Country needs a goddamn wake-up call. Wall Street jerk-offs stealing people's money—paid-off dickwads in Congress paving the way. Jesus H. Christ on a surfboard! Makes you mad enough to wanna blow something up—send a message." Quentin appeared locked in, riveted to his every word.

"I can just picture it in the movie. Ba-boom! In the name of 300 million pissed-off Americans. Too bad no one in real life has the stones to make it happen." Now Quentin's eyes had narrowed and vertical ridges appeared in his forehead. "I mean, it's one thing to sit around sipping our beers or some fine scotch talking about sticking it to the man— might make us feel important for a couple minutes—but in the end we know it's all talk. Am I right, lieutenant?" Stan glanced back at Charles and snuck in a grin.

Silence now hanging heavy in the enclosed cabin, Quentin guided the aircraft toward the shipyard. His lips seemed to twitch but his mouth did not open. If you could cut a man open just by staring at him, Stan would need a medic right about now. "OK, Mr. Bullshit

Apocalypse Wannabe. What would you do?" said Quentin. "Hypothetically speaking, of course."

"Hmm, good question. Nuke plant, shipyard—it's not like we don't live in a target-rich environment. But that concrete dome is thicker than my goddamn skull. And the shipyard, after that fire they had there back in oh-twelve, you gotta believe that place is locked down tighter than a drill instructor's anus."

The fire Stan was referring to—just before his scatological metaphor invoking the anatomy of a tightly wound military training officer—was a 2012 incident in which a twenty-four-year-old civilian painter/sandblaster started a small blaze in a nuclear submarine in hopes of getting out of work early. The moron's arson scheme racked up a half-million-dollar repair bill before the Navy ultimately decided to scrap the sub.

"OK. First I'd pay fifty bucks to some pimply faced hacker to crash some vulnerable power grid. Then maybe pull out some vintage ricin or anthrax from my biological weapons cellar. Release a little taste of it, then threaten to fuck up a major city every 12 hours until they meet my demands," said Stan.

"I'd pay another teenager, maybe the same kid, to get my manifesto viral on social media. Seriously, you gotta have a manifesto nowadays. I'd probably play up the disgruntled Vietnam vet angle to drum up more headlines, maybe threaten to throw in an AK-47 rampage just cause I'm a big fan of overkill. But that's just off the top of my head— haven't really thought it through. What about you?"

"Well, first of all I'd probably neutralize any smart-ass little bitch who tried to jerk me around by questioning the size of my *cojones*," Quentin fired back.

"Ha! Ha! Ha!" Stan was not a man to be easily intimidated. "No need to get riled up, lieutenant. I know they cut your nuts off before you could fly your chopper into the Pentagon back in the 70s, so I was just trying to see what kind of state of mind you're in today."

Quentin flinched hard, causing the chopper to dip and shake. Stan's shoot-from-the-lip, "taunt the psychopath" strategy had clearly escalated things to a "shit's getting real" level. But instead of feeling scared, Charles was jazzed— invigorated by the sensation that his brain's "danger zone" synapses were twitching like mad.

"Hey, this is awesome," he said, trying to ease the throttle on the insanity that was ricocheting around the tiny cockpit. "Solid material for the book. I knew you guys would have great… synergy." Quentin changed course and began piloting the chopper past the Memorial Bridge and back toward Market Square.

Chapter 43

Charles could still see blue lights flashing in the neighborhood of the five-story brick federal building that housed the post office and a dozen or so U.S. Government offices ranging from the FBI and the ATF to the IRS and the Social Security Administration.

Quentin, now mute, was making a beeline for the building. Charles' mind downshifted into slow motion as a sickening sixth sense stabbed at his gut.

This is the target!

The revelation brought a sense of sheer horror as he realized that, not only were the lives of dozens, perhaps hundreds of people in imminent peril, Keri Ann was inside. He thought of the letter he had written to her. His instinct to compose it in the past tense now seemed prescient, the only copy in his left breast pocket, inches away from the Beretta.

"Hey Quentin, what are we doing here? You forget to mail your manifesto?" If he was, in fact, intent on hitting the federal building, Charles was determined to knock him off stride, buy a little time. Stan laughed, but Quentin looked serious. "Good one," he said. "Nope, wish I'd thought of Stan's social media idea. But I guess I'm old school. Dropped a dozen copies in the mail yesterday. Handed them off to your girlfriend, in fact. The pretty little blonde."

Finally, it seemed that all the pretenses of ball-busting and book-writing were stripped away as Charles and Stan both realized that the man holding the controls of the helicopter, dangling their lives in front of their faces, was not fabricating a blueprint for a fictional terror plot, he was carrying out a real one. Quentin was smiling again, as if after a few moments of unexpectedly antagonistic banter, the protagonist was now totally back in control. "You fucking amateurs really don't know who you're dealing with, do you?"

"OK, I guess we underestimated you," said Charles, who had in fact been trying to figure out who the fuck he was dealing with since the day he had answered the "Help wanted: Ghostwriter" ad.

"Damn right you did. And now you're sitting in a chopper carrying a special cargo, rigged to inflict maximum American carnage," said Quentin. "I even timed an email inviting the police and some of their friends to our little party so we could beef up the death toll with some first responders." Quentin was gleefully confirming their worst suspicions; even so, Charles and Stan were stunned. "Nothing serious enough to evacuate the building, of course," said Quentin. "I just told them some idiot was causing a disturbance at the IRS because his accountant said he couldn't claim his tropical fish tank as a deduction on his tax return."

"Not too late to reconsider," said Charles. "You've got a helluva novel on your hands. Why not send your message that way instead of killing a bunch of innocent people?" Quentin laughed so hard and with such maniacal enthusiasm that Charles actually thought it felt a little forced, as if he was hamming it up to underscore his own archvillain mythology.

"I wasn't really writing a novel, morons. But they're definitely gonna be writing some stories about our little adventure here today. Ha ha ha!"

Quentin's mad euphoria caused spittle to fly from his mouth and Stan to wipe a speck of it from beneath his left eye. "Congratulations, bitches. The names Charles Manson Smith and Apocalypse Nowell are going down in history as accomplices of the infamous guerrilla terrorist Lt. Roger Quentin!"

As Quentin aimed the chopper in a downward trajectory toward a big window on the building's fifth floor, Stan lunged for him, grabbing for the cyclic and the collective lever. The aircraft jolted upward and pitched wildly amid the turbulence, as the two men wrestled for control of the aircraft. Charles grabbed Quentin from behind, trying to strangle him, but ended up boxing him in the ear with his left hand while his right index and middle fingers became lodged in the pilot's mouth.

"Faarrgghh you," shouted Quentin. Stan got the speeding

chopper pointed back toward the bridge and seconds later they were lurching at dangerously low altitude over the river. Flailing, Quentin finally connected with Stan's head and sent him crashing into the door, knocking it open. As Stan sprung back, Quentin hammered him with a kick that sent him tumbling out of the cabin, where he grabbed onto one of the skids and hung on, dangling above the water.

Dazed but back in control, Quentin glanced back to see Charles pointing the Beretta at his head. "You haven't got the guts." Quentin was sneering at him as Charles smashed the butt end of the gun into his skull, just above his left temple. His head snapped in response to the blow, but the gun was too small to administer a proper pistol-whipping and Quentin started laughing that stupid fake evil genius laugh again.

Charles exhaled hard and fired one shot into Quentin's back. The pilot slumped over as the helicopter nicked the top of the bridge and broke apart, and then exploded a split second before crashing into the surface of the swift-flowing Piscataqua.

Chapter 44

The Coast Guard rescue vessel fished Stan out of the water first, about fifty yards from the Maine side of the river. He was easy to find, bobbing in the current, cursing like a soldier.

A photographer from the paper was on the scene almost immediately as onlookers began perching themselves on piers, wharves, balconies and the bridge, which somehow had escaped major damage, craning to see the smoking chopper sinking into the river. Police closed the bridge to vehicular traffic and began trying to shoo people back to shore when a burly man in a thick Carhartt coat yelled, "I see a body!"

Quentin was floating face-down when a young seaman hauled him aboard the twenty-five-foot Coast Guard response boat. He would be pronounced dead forty-five minutes later at Coastal Hospital, a bullet wound in his back and burns covering much of his face and neck.

Stan, soaked and wrapped in a survival blanket, resisted the urge to stand up, rush over to Quentin and kick the death out of him with his heavy boots. But minutes passed and Quentin still wasn't moving. "That lifeless piece of shit is Lt. Roger Quentin," Stan told the officer in charge. "He was trying to fly his helicopter into the federal building. My friend Charles was in that chopper. I heard a shot. You gotta find him."

The search continued for several hours—Coast Guard, Marine Patrol, State Police and local authorities scanning the water from the air, from the shore and from the tall interstate bridge further upriver. A TV news van arrived and set up its equipment for a live feed, shooting toward the bridge from nearby Prescott Park.

Watching the news at home with a cup of tea, her feet curled under a blanket and Bailey by her side, was Keri Ann.

"One local man is dead, another remains missing and a third is in stable condition at Coastal Hospital this evening after a helicopter exploded and crashed into the Piscataqua River in what law enforcement sources say was a domestic terror plot gone wrong. We now go live to Brent Phillips, who is on the ground at the scene of the blast."

"Well John, in a scene that reads like something right out of a bizarre Hollywood thriller, authorities are continuing the search for an unemployed local man named Charles Manson Smith—yes, you heard correctly, Charles Manson Smith— who, according to one eyewitness, may have sacrificed his own life to foil one of the most ambitious, and outlandish, home-grown terror plots ever to unfold in American airspace."

Keri Ann dropped her mug and Bailey scampered off the couch and out of the room. She grabbed the remote and turned up the volume, as pictures of Charles and another man appeared side by side on the screen.

"Killed in the helicopter crash was Lt. Roger Quentin, a wealthy, eccentric retired police officer and military veteran, who Homeland Security officials are calling the mastermind behind the thwarted attack. As police continue to figure out exactly what happened, the only known survivor of the crash, a Vietnam veteran named Stanley 'Apocalypse' Nowell, is claiming that after he was thrown from the chopper, Mr. Smith narrowly prevented the pilot from blowing up the federal building in a suicide mission. To characterize the whole scene as something stranger than fiction would be an understatement. One first responder I spoke to described it as something out of a James Patterson novel with a touch of Stephen King. We'll bring you more details just as soon as they are available."

"Thank you, Brent. When we return..." Keri Ann was frozen, unable to move anything more than her right thumb. She tried to flip to another channel to learn more.

A Fox News personality was saying something about Joe Biden and the socialist radical left destroying America. MSNBC had a clip of Greta Thunberg begging world leaders not to destroy the planet. TMZ was promising exclusive breaking news about the controversy involving the latest short-lived celebrity marriage gone haywire. Mr. Krabs was firing SpongeBob SquarePants from his job on Nickelodeon. IFC was screening *The Shining.*

She buried her face in her hands and began to cry as Bailey hopped back onto the sofa and nuzzled her left arm.

Chapter 45

Charles felt bruises and swelling all over his neck. He hoisted himself into a seated position, his ribcage delivering sharp jolts of pain with each movement. His entire body ached, especially his neck. In the moonlight, he could see that his left hand had suffered burns, but his right hand had not. He could also see that he was missing his left shoe.

He did not know where he was, but he knew it was very important that he feed his cat. He also theorized that, since one of his first impulses was to get home and feed the cat, he had likely taken a serious blow to the head. He found further evidence of this while gingerly examining the tender, charcoal briquette-sized lump behind his left ear.

He tried to say "what the fuck?" but no words came out. For a moment, Charles was unsure if he was deaf or mute. The church clock began to chime in the distance. OK, not deaf. He figured his inability to speak must be connected to the welt on his skull and the likelihood that he might be in a state of shock.

The church clock chimed again. He squinted into the

darkness in the direction of the tower bell, but could not yet determine where he was.

Three. The sound of water lapping softly against a hard surface meant he was near the river, but where?

Four. He could smell fish and feel cool grass beneath his hands. Far edge of the park near the fishing pier?

Five. A searchlight swept from a boat in the middle of the channel past his position on the shore.

Six. Downtown must be that way. He tried to rise but fell back down.

Seven. Jesus! His mind suddenly flashed to Quentin and Stan in the helicopter. A gunshot. Then darkness. He strained to reach for his holster and found it empty.

Eight. Quentin's laugh. The post office. Keri Ann! The letter was still in his pocket—damp, probably ruined.

Nine. He remembered the struggle, Stan tumbling out of the chopper. It must have crashed into the river.

Ten. He knew he had tried to stop Quentin, but the rest was a blank. He must have dragged himself ashore and passed out. He wondered if Stan and Quentin were somewhere nearby.

Eleven. He had to get help. Charles struggled to his feet and started limping toward Market Square.

Chapter 46

"The police found him a little after midnight, blacked out by the front door of the station. An officer revived him, but they said he couldn't speak. Or wouldn't." Stan was at Charles' bedside in the hospital, speaking to Keri Ann who was standing on the other side as a nurse replaced the IV while pretending not to listen. A federal agent sat rigid in a nearby chair, listening to every word.

"Charlie, can you hear me?" Stan gently grasped his friend's left arm, above the white bandages that covered his hand.

"Charles, it's me," said Keri Ann, her right hand resting on top of his. Charles slowly opened his eyes. "Nurse, he's awake," said Keri Ann. "Charles, are you alright?" Seeing her there, feeling her hand on his, moved Charles almost to tears. But he did not speak. "We're here," she nodded her head across the bed to Stan.

Charles squinted at Stan. His head was pounding, but his thoughts were becoming clearer. *What about Quentin, you asshole? Did it occur to you that I might want to know whether the madman whose chopper we crashed into the river—the guy I shot, for chrissake—is dead or alive?* Charles pulled a groan from deep in his thorax, still unable to speak.

"He's dead," said Stan. "Quentin is dead. Bullet through the chest and a burnt-up head. You did it, buddy. You got that son of a bitch. The police and a whole crew of feds are waiting to talk to you." Charles' eyes narrowed in pain as he tried to gesture toward his throat. "It's OK," said Keri Ann. "The doctors told them you might not be able to speak for a while."

Screw the doctors. Eff the police, he thought, editing the profanity from his internal dialogue in her presence. *I can't believe you're here, standing next to me, caring about me.* He was crying inside, but could not tell if his tears were visible.

Dear Keri Ann... he searched his mind to quote from his note—the saltwater-drenched letter in which he had, with great difficulty, organized his feelings and tried to pour out his heart.

As you know, certain aspects of my personality make it extremely hard, if not physically impossible, for me to communicate openly about matters involving interpersonal intimacy.

Seriously? So poetic, he thought, already slamming his own painstaking efforts to express himself to her, as he converted his memory of those thoughtfully composed sentiments into a silent message to the woman standing at his side.

How I wish that I could look into your beautiful green eyes and just tell you... Reach deep into my soul, overcome the inhibitions and voices that warn me to keep quiet, and just find the words to tell you... Words that I fear will frighten you because our friendship is just beginning... Words I have never before spoken to another human being... Words that, even though it is impossible for me to love myself, are the only ones I know to express how strongly I feel about you, Keri Ann.

"We'll let you rest now," she said. "Stan's getting discharged and he's going to take me to your house so we can feed Elmer and get you some supplies. We'll leave the TV on for you."

After they left the room, Charles tapped at the channel button on the remote. The agent had disappeared from his chair.

"*...the latest on Tuesday's foiled helicopter terror plot. Authorities say the alleged terrorist killed in the crash, Lt. Roger Quentin, had hired Charles Manson Smith, an unemployed former journalist now recuperating from undisclosed injuries at a local hospital, to ghostwrite a book for him. Police and Homeland Security officials reportedly received a manifesto attributed to Quentin and described as a rambling anti-government diatribe filled with profane and colorful language under the heading The Madman Cometh...*"

The newsflash continued: "*...law enforcement sources have so far remained mum about Mr. Smith's account of the events, but eyewitness Stanley 'Apocalypse' Nowell, a local*

Vietnam veteran who was thrown from the chopper just moments before the crash, is hailing his friend as a hero…" Charles, who had been gazing out the window during the report, looked back when he heard footsteps and saw a stocky disheveled poltergeist reaching up to click off the television.

"Hero." Richard Smith spit out the H-word as if it were an obscenity. "Unemployed journalist mental case—ghostwriting a manifesto for a fucking terrorist. What a disgrace."

The contempt oozing from his father's jaw sounded as bitter and virulent as it had the last time he'd heard that voice well over 30 years ago. It summoned up a visceral hate cloud of scorn—saturated with ghosts and skeletons wielding clenched fists and brickbats, raw X-rays of a fractured spirit, smoke-tinged flashbacks of unfinished filicide—that nearly suffocated him in his hospital bed.

Charles' entire body tightened as the older man walked toward the bed. His face appeared corroded from within by subsurface bile, his cloudy yellow-brown eyes flickering with revulsion and malevolence.

"What do you have to say for yourself—Charles. Manson. Smith?" The words slithered from his mouth, sodden with 40-proof saliva and stale venom. Charles glared back at him, fuming inside. The cardiac monitor seemed to give a yelp as his heart rate spiked, yet he felt strangely calm. The invective he had crafted and rehearsed to be ready if this moment ever arrived… suddenly felt hollow. He reached down into his gut and forced himself to speak.

"Ummph. Father. Hoped I'd never see you again. But glad you're here." Then, just to mess with his head, Charles mustered a weak smile as he choked out three words.

"I… love… you."

His father's eyes darkened, his face twisted into a grimace from the blunt impact of the invisible slap. He recoiled, staggered and flopped to the floor, his head snapping back and slamming onto the hard tile surface. Charles muscled his upper body up onto his elbows, leaned over the edge of his hospital bed and saw the lifeless form of his old man sprawled beneath him. He took a slow, deep breath and tilted his head while trying to puzzle out the strange sensation he was experiencing. It felt something like… peace.

Charles Manson Smith laid his head back down. Clutched a second pillow close to his heart. And closed his eyes.

About the Author

A writer since birth, **John Breneman** has mad stories to tell as he hurtles headlong into the next chapter of life. Currently employed as a senior marketing copywriter/editor, he is a multi-decade newspaper journalist (reporter, editor, columnist, page designer, etc.) and the author of *Downsized! How I Got Laid Off After 30 Years in Newspapers and Turned My Funniest Sunday Advice Columns into a Blockbuster E-book*.

He is also the founder and CEO of Triple Action Enterprises, which he refers to as "a virtual multinational Imagination Factory conglomerate with rich Intellectual Property Holdings across the Universal Spectrum of Creative Expression about The Human Experience in a World Gone Haywire." *A Man of Remarkable Restraint* is his debut novel.

If you enjoyed reading this book,
please consider writing your honest review
and sharing it with other readers.

Many of our Authors are happy to participate in
Book Club and Reader Group discussions.
For more information, contact us at info@encirclepub.com.

Thank you,
Encircle Publications

For news about more exciting new fiction, join us at:

Facebook: www.facebook.com/encirclepub

Instagram: www.instagram.com/encirclepublications

Twitter: twitter.com/encirclepub

Sign up for Encircle Publications newsletter and specials:
eepurl.com/cs8taP